Megan reached out and put a mittened hand on Adam's cheek.

"I think we're making progress, don't you?" she asked.

Adam placed his hand on hers and removed it from his face. She cursed her impulse to touch him, breaking her own rules. She tucked her hands in her lap while he closed the passenger door and walked around the truck to get in on the other side. He started the engine and turned in the seat to look at her. "Megan, I appreciate you trying to make inroads for me in the community."

She grinned. "Maybe you deserve a second chance."

"Maybe?" He raised one eyebrow then cracked a smile.

"I've discovered that you really have changed from that bully I remember. You've become a good man."

"Don't glamorize it. I'm far from good." He put the truck in gear and pulled away from the curb, steering back toward the bank.

"You're working hard to make amends. Isn't that what a good man would do?"

Dear Reader,

Bullying seems to be a hot topic right now, although that behavior has been around for years. I was bullied in fourth grade. It never got physical, but the verbal taunts made me feel as if I'd been punched. It affected my self-esteem as well as my physical well-being, and I missed a lot of school days due to stomach issues that year. I was grateful when my bully graduated into middle school the following term.

The issue of bullying plays into Megs's and Adam's lives in this story. Megs lost a friend because of bullying, and she blames herself for what happened. The what-ifs haunt her. What if she had stood up to the bully sooner? But what if she had stayed silent? Adam was a bully in high school who is now back in his hometown to hopefully make up for his past. He has learned to be a better man, but the specter of his bullying past follows him still. Theirs is a compelling romance.

My hope is that my story will spark conversations about bullying and how to protect our children and that it will shed some light on this issue from several different points of view.

Syndi

HEARTWARMING

The Sweetheart Deal

Syndi Powell

ISBN-13: 978-0-373-36780-1

The Sweetheart Deal

This edition published by arrangement with Harlequin Books S.A.

For questions and comments about the quality of this book, please contact us at CustomerService@Harlequin.com.

Printed in U.S.A.

Syndi Powell started writing stories when she was young and has made it a lifelong pursuit. She's been reading Harlequin romance novels since she was in her teens and is thrilled to be on the Harlequin team. She loves to connect with readers on Twitter, @syndipowell, or on her Facebook author page, Facebook.com/syndipowellauthor.

Books by Syndi Powell

Harlequin Heartwarming

The Reluctant Bachelor
Risk of Falling
Two-Part Harmony

This book is dedicated to my nieces and nephews: Sam, Jack, Page and Penny Hartman; and Shelby, Megan and Zach Skrzypczak. Thank you for making me feel like a supercool rock star every time I come over to see you. Crazy Aunt Syndi loves you all. And if I haven't written "your" story, don't worry. It's coming.

PROLOGUE

MEGAN SWEET RAN down the sidewalk past the shops on Lincoln Street and opened the door to the Sweetheart bakery. Stepping inside, she took a deep breath and savored for a moment the scents of yeast and sugar that filled the air. Grammy stood behind the counter refilling the glass display case with cookies. She glanced up at Megs and paused in her work. "Honey, what is it? What's wrong?"

Megs shook her head, unable to put into words the mix of emotions that flooded her heart. "Kenny, he's..." She hung her head and closed her eyes. "Grammy, he's dead."

Grammy came around the counter and enveloped her in a tight hug. Megs rested her head against her grandmother's ample chest and felt the first tears start to leak from her eyes.

"I wasn't sure if you'd heard yet." Grammy stroked her hair. "Are you okay?"

Megs raised her head and stared into Grammy's hazel-brown eyes, much like her own. "How can I be? He was my best friend. And now he's gone. What am I going to do?"

The front door opened, and two customers walked in. Grammy greeted them, then escorted Megs into the kitchen. She pulled out a stool and motioned to Megs to sit down. "I'll help these ladies, then I'll be right back."

Megs hopped up on the stool and stared at her hands folded in her lap. She should have kept her mouth shut. She should have let the bully say and do what he wanted. But no, she'd had to stand up to him, and now Kenny was dead.

The swinging doors opened, and Grammy stepped into the kitchen. Megs expected her to talk, to assure her that everything would be okay. Instead, she pulled out an old recipe ledger and flipped through the pages. She finally settled on a page and pointed it out to Megs. "Here we are. This cookie helps to soothe a worried soul." Grammy chose an apron from a shelf and tossed it at Megs. "Put it on. You're going to make these on your own."

Megs raised an eyebrow at this. She'd helped her grandmother make cookies before, but it had never been suggested that she bake them solo. She slipped the apron over her head, then wound the strings around her waist before tying them in front. "But I don't know this recipe."

"You can't always rely on what you know." Grammy nudged the ledger toward her. "Follow the recipe. Trust in yourself. It will guide you."

She started to gather the ingredients: flour, sugar, butter and eggs. And the tin of dark cocoa. Megs lifted the lid and took a deep breath. Ambrosia.

As Grammy watched, she carefully measured and sifted, creamed and mixed. She referred back to the ledger when she doubted the next step, and later suppressed a smile when the dough formed into a ball exactly like it should. She glanced at her grandmother, who beamed at her. "You're a natural, Megs. Like me."

The next step was to let the dough firm

up in the refrigerator for a half hour, so Megs put the mixing bowl in the walk-in cooler and returned to the warm kitchen. Grammy held out a mug of tea to her. "I know that Kenny's death doesn't make sense. Suicide never does. But he'll always have a special place in your heart. And as long as you hold on to that, at least he can live on in your memories."

Megs cupped her hands around the mug and let the warmth extend down her fingers toward her arms. "I'm afraid that I wasn't a very good friend to him lately."

Grammy wrapped her arms around her and squeezed her tight. "I doubt that. You're the best friend any person could ask for." She tweaked the end of her nose. "After all, you're the best granddaughter. One of them, at least."

When the half hour was over, Megs rolled out the dough, then used a knife to cut it into strips. She twisted them into shapes before placing them on a buttered cookie sheet, then slipped them into the oven. She leaned against the marble worktable and crossed her arms over her chest. "Will it ever stop hurting like this?"

Grammy nodded. "One day, it won't hurt as much. But you'll always miss him." She gave a soft smile. "I still miss your grandfather. And your dad."

"Me, too."

"But the pain's gotten easier, isn't that right?" She put a hand on Megs's shoulder. "It will be the same with Kenny."

When the timer went off, Megs used a pot holder to bring out the sheet of twists and placed it on the counter. She grabbed a metal spatula to hold out one of the cookies. Grammy took it and bit into it. Megs watched as she chewed, then relaxed when she smiled.

"You did good." Grammy finished the cookie and peered at Megs. "One day, this place will belong to you. All my recipes and the business, too. And you will learn to feed people's souls as well as their bodies. Just like me."

At that moment, there was nothing Megs wanted more.

CHAPTER ONE

MEGS RESTED HER hand on the old recipe ledger, missing Grammy even more today than ever before. Had it really been four months already since she had died? It didn't seem possible.

She shook off her grief and glanced at the clock. It was a little after four in the morning, her favorite time of the day, just before her employees arrived, when the bakery she had inherited belonged to her alone. She flipped through the pages of the ledger, looking for the right recipe. She needed something special. Something that would shake the dark foreboding that sat heavily on her shoulders.

With the radio blaring, Megs sang along as she creamed the butter and sugar. A strange sound made her look up, but only for a moment. Then she was sifting the flour into the butter mixture, beating the silver cup with the side of her hand.

Though many of her customers loved their standbys, she liked to introduce new items every once in a while. Sometimes to good reviews, others to less than stellar. Hopefully, these butter cookies would inspire new beginnings just like Grammy had promised in the ledger.

Another weird groan came from above her, then a crack as if ice were breaking. She glanced at the ceiling and frowned. One fleeting thought sprang to mind: *Get under the table.* She hugged the ledger to her chest and scooted beneath the worktable just before the roof gave way.

COLD. SO COLD. Megs peeked from under the table and saw chunks of ice and snow amid roof shingles and splintered wood littering the floor of the kitchen. She remained where she was, however, unsure of whether there would be more falling debris. She hoped not. She hoped this didn't mean the end of the Sweetheart.

Megs tried not to cry. Would someone hear her if she did? She called out, but it was so early. Who else was up this early? "Help!" she hollered again. "I'm under here!" Only silence followed. She thrust her hands into the pockets of her jeans, but she'd left her phone in her jacket, which was across the room. Out of reach.

Minutes passed. How long had she been under here? She wasn't sure anymore. It felt like hours, but it couldn't be. Didn't matter, her back was cramping badly. Shivers raced down her spine. Staying here for much longer wasn't an option. She tested her feet, her legs, her arms. Mentally checking if she was all right. She seemed to be. She could be grateful for that at least.

Grateful? How could she—

Was that…

The sirens of the fire trucks and police cars already. "Don't worry," she whispered, clutching the ledger tighter to her chest. "They're coming. Everything will be fine now."

Oh, how she wanted to believe those words.

ADAM HAWKINS'S PHONE rang twice before he had reached the bank. Because of the precarious conditions of the roads, he ignored it and continued on his way. He needed to get in early so he could get the sidewalks shoveled before customers arrived. He'd already called to ensure the plows had reached his parking lot, but the sidewalks were his responsibility. Welcome to small-town Northern Michigan.

As much as he hated to admit it, returning to his hometown as bank manager was pretty gratifying. The people in town hadn't thought he'd grow up to be much more than a thug, but he'd shown them. He'd become respectable, even wore a suit and tie. A man that his father should be proud of.

Not that anyone seemed to have noticed the internal change in him. Not even his parents, who lived in the same town, but still refused to see him. They still saw the bully, though dressed in a suit. He pulled into the bank parking lot near the back, grabbed the shovel he'd stowed in the bed of his truck and walked carefully to the snow mounded on the sidewalks. Within minutes, he had a square foot of cement cleaned off and felt ready to quit and hire someone else to shovel the rest. Despite the deceptive white fluffy appearance, the snow was wet and heavy. His heart thumped loudly in his chest and his arms ached. Still, only thirty minutes remained until his employees would show, then another thirty for his first customers.

Another car belonging to his teller Eva Stone arrived at the parking lot. When she got out of her car, she looked as though she had dressed for Alaska. She was wearing a thick parka with a hood fringed with faux fur, two scarves wound around her neck and fat mittens on her hands. She approached him slowly, carrying a shovel. She leaned back to look up into his face since she only reached halfway to his shoulder. "Did you hear about the roofs collapsing downtown?"

Leave it to one of his employees to have the latest scoop. "What roofs?"

"Several businesses on Lincoln are gone." She shook her head then started to shovel small loads of snow. "It's too bad about the Sweetheart."

Adam stared across the parking lot toward town. Megan, the baker, was a client of the bank's both professionally and personally. He wondered if she was okay, then reminded himself that she seemed to want nothing to do with him since his return to Lake Mildred. When he ordered pastries for the staff meetings, her sister or another employee delivered them. The night he had stopped in to the bakery himself, she'd stayed in the kitchen for his entire visit until he'd left with his bread. And she never came by his office at the bank when she made her deposits. "Yes, too bad. What other businesses?"

"Will wasn't sure of the extent of the damage, but it's huge." She pushed the snow to the edge of the curb and leaned on her shovel. "The apartments, too. Lot of people homeless this morning."

Adam put his hand on Eva's shoulder. "You don't have to shovel the snow. I can take care of this."

"You saying I can't?"

The spark in her eyes made him wince. "No!" He cleared his throat and started over. "Once we get the snow cleared from the front door, I'd like you to get the branch ready for the day. Coffee brewed, hot water for tea. We're sure to have a lot of visitors today."

"I can shovel snow, too. I'm not an invalid."

He'd seen proof of that himself. He held up a hand. "Didn't say you were."

"Despite what my son says..." She continued to shovel the snow, and together they cleared a path to the door. She paused as Adam unlocked the front doors. Once opened, she disappeared inside. He glanced around the parking lot, then bent his head and continued shoveling the sidewalk.

Finally finished, he shook the snow off himself, then entered the branch. He sniffed appreciatively and walked through the lobby, down the hall to the staff room. Eva turned and handed him a cup of hot coffee. "Black, two sugars."

"You're too good to me, Eva."

"Someone has to take care of you bachelors." She took a sip of her own tea, then nodded to the thermoses on the counter. "I made extra if you want to deliver them to the emergency workers downtown. I'm sure they could use a hot drink right about now. Do wonders for the bank's image, no?"

Adam nodded. When he'd taken the branch manager position, he'd inherited a mess both financially and publicly. The previous manager had been responsible for foreclosing on many homes in the area, known for his tough stance rather than his compassion. Adam's district manager had warned him what he was walking into. Add that to his own past problems with the residents, and Eva was right. Giving out coffee would be only the beginning of what he needed to do. "I'll drop them off as soon as Sandy arrives. Great idea, Eva."

She tapped her head. "Got a bunch of them locked up here."

Later that morning, Adam bundled up and once again trekked out into the frigid landscape. He carried the two thermoses and a plastic bag full of cups, stirrers and packets of cream and sugar. When he reached the corner of Main and Lincoln, he paused. It looked as if a bomb had exploded. He moved to the barricades and motioned to one of the workers. "I brought you guys coffee."

Keith walked over. "Thanks, man."

"Anyone get trapped?"

"They're getting the baker out now. She was there when the roof collapsed. And they're still digging some of the tenants out at the apartments. In a weird way, it's a good thing it happened so early in the morning. Less people around to get hurt."

Adam closed his eyes at the thought of Megan trapped under snow and ice. She had to be okay.

Keith gave a grin. "I'm going to miss her double-chocolate muffins though. Those got me through many a shift."

"How long do you think it will take to get this cleaned up?"

Keith looked back and shrugged. "Day or two. But longer to rebuild." He accepted the thermoses and bags. "Appreciate it."

"Courtesy of the bank."

The man seemed to wince a little but returned to his crew with the coffee. Several turned to Adam and yelled their thanks. He nodded and turned to go back to the bank.

And then he saw her.

Megan emerged from the bakery, a blanket wrapped around her shoulders, and ambled between two emergency workers. Her sister ran to her and put her arms around her. She didn't look as if she'd been badly injured. He hoped she wasn't.

Before now he hadn't noticed that the Sweetheart was smack-dab in the middle of the most damage. He thought of the bank where he'd be needed. But his feet betrayed him as he walked slowly until he stood in front of her. "I'm sorry about the Sweetheart, Megan. But I'm glad you're all right."

She glanced up sharply at him then shifted away. Her sister, Kelly, rolled her eyes. "I'll bet you're sorry. Go find someone else to harass."

Okay, maybe he'd deserved that before, but he'd changed. He reached into his pocket and pulled out a business card. "When you're ready to discuss rebuilding..."

Megan looked at the card held out to her, then after many long seconds, she took it and put it in the pocket of her jeans. Never saying a word.

Adam turned and almost bumped into a man. He apologized, then paused. He didn't need to ask if the man he'd almost knocked down was Bobby Snow or not since he looked much the same. He still wore glasses, and the chubbiness of adolescence had remained. Bobby recognized him, too, as he made to leave. Adam followed him, however, weaving through the crowd of people who had come to witness the destruction. Adam called after him, "Wait, Bobby. I just want to talk to you."

"Leave me the hell alone."

"I want to apologize."

The other man stopped and faced Adam. "You're joking, right?" He turned to see if anyone else in the crowd was listening to him. "Is this guy kidding me? Because an apology won't make up for what you did."

"I was a jerk in high school. I'm sorry for the awful things I said and did to you."

"Such as..." Bobby crossed his arms over his chest.

Adam pinched the bridge of his nose. "You really want a list? Fine. I'm sorry for shoving you into the girls' restroom about once a week for three years. I'm sorry that I called you Piggy and Fatty and oinked when you walked down the hall at school." He started counting things off on his fingers. "I apologize for stealing your lunch. For having Sarah McGillis write you a love letter as a joke. For having my team members TP your house. And your car."

"You made Sarah write that note?" Bobby shook his head. "Of course you did. You hated me, so why not humiliate me?"

"I'm sorry." Adam sighed. "I want to apologize and see if I can do anything to make it up to you."

"Why?"

His other victims always asked that question, and he'd never been able to come up with the right answer. "Because I hate how I treated you when we were in high school. You didn't deserve it, and I'm sorry."

Bobby looked him over. "What can you possibly do to atone for making my life miserable for four years?"

Adam shifted his weight from side to side. This was always the hardest part. Because how could he make up for that? For some, it was easy to lend them a helping hand. Others let him off the hook without requiring anything. But Bobby seemed to be the type that would never forgive him no matter what. "What do you want, Bobby? How can I make this up to you?"

Bobby started to laugh, and people started

to stare at them. "You really think you can do something to change the stuff that happened twelve years ago? That was the time to make amends. Not now." He hesitated then shook his head again. "Forget it."

He started to walk away, but Adam reached out and grabbed his arm. "Please. There's got to be something."

"You can't change what happened with us, but if you really want to do something you can go talk to the kids in high school like me who have bullies like you. Better yet, you can tell the entire high school how bullying turned you into a big shot while your victims suffered humiliation beyond high school, and worse, died."

Adam paled and dropped his hand. He was right.

Bobby waved him off. "You're all talk, but when it comes to action, you've got nothing. I don't accept your apology. Now you can live with that."

And he spun on his heel and left Adam among the crowd, who eyed him warily. He'd done what he came to do, so Adam took his leave and tromped through the snow heading to the bank. So much rebuilding was left to do in this town.

And the easiest part would be the buildings. The attitudes and memories would take much longer.

THE PARAMEDIC REMOVED the blood pressure cuff and nodded at Megs. "Your pressure is a little elevated, but that's understandable. There's no need to insist you go to the hospital, but I recommend taking it easy the rest of the day."

Megs agreed. "Not as if I can go back to work."

Her sister, Kelly, handed her a jacket she'd brought with her since Megs's was buried under rubble. "We should go home. There's nothing more we can do here."

Megs slowly walked away from the ambulance toward the crowd gathered to watch the crew pull down part of the standing back wall. She blinked away the tears that froze in the frigid wind. "You go ahead. I'm staying."

Her sister's boyfriend, Sam, put a hand on her shoulder. "It won't help, Megs. Let the workers do what they have to, and I'll go in with you tomorrow when they give us the all-clear."

How could you go in something that no longer had a roof and four walls? Her heart was heavy. She teared up again.

Kelly and Sam watched her intently until finally she couldn't stand it any longer. "Listen, I'm cold and I'm hungry. We could go get something to eat, but then I'm coming straight back. I can't go home. Not yet."

Kelly offered her a hopeful smile. "Fine. But if you're staying, I am, too." To Sam, she said, "I'm not going anywhere without her."

He put his arms around her sister and kissed the top of her hat. "I know you won't. We'll all stay."

He steered both sisters down the street toward Rick's diner. They had to wait several minutes for a table to open up since it seemed everyone had the same idea: get warmth and food before heading back to the disaster on Lincoln. When they managed to claim a window booth that overlooked Main, Megs stared at the menu but didn't really see the words. Not that she needed to see what was there to know what was listed. She'd spent many mealtimes in the diner since her mother had left them after her father died thirteen years ago. She shook away the emptiness that settled over her at the thought of Grammy. *Oh, Grammy, you'd hate to see the Sweetheart today.*

At least what was left of it.

She looked up to find Kelly peering at her over the top of her menu. Her sister lowered it and reached across the table to grab her hand. "Grammy would be feeling exactly what you are right now. I know it."

Megs doubted it. Because she felt as if she was mourning Grammy all over again. First to lose her beloved grandmother and mentor, and now her business, too? If Grammy was here…

But she wasn't.

Kelly's blue eyes filled with tears. "If something had happened to you…" She took a big gulp and wiped at the corner of her eyes.

Megs squeezed her hand. "I know. But I'm fine."

The waitress arrived to take their orders.

Megs ordered some soup and coffee, the hotter the better to get her warmed up before returning to the frigid climes. Shirley grimaced when she asked for the bread basket. "Well, we didn't get our bakery order this morning, so we have bread that Rick bought from the grocery store. The rolls aren't the same as yours, but..."

Right. Because Megs hadn't been able to bake and deliver their daily order without the bakery. The loss of the Sweetheart extended beyond her. Something to remember as she made plans to rebuild. Because she had to rebuild, right? People and businesses depended on her. "I'll still take the bread basket, Shirley. Thanks."

The waitress nodded and left their table to put in their orders. Sam sighed. "I'm going to miss your crullers the most, I think."

"I can still make some for you at home." Because that would be the only place she could use ovens until the bakery would reopen. "It will keep me busy at least while I wait."

Sam held up his coffee cup. "We could look at this as something terrible. Or we could see this as a chance for you to fashion the Sweetheart in your own image. I can build it better than it was before."

"What about Grammy's house?" His offer was generous to say the least, but Sam and Kelly had been remodeling Grammy's turn-of-the-century farmhouse for months. While the first floor was completed, they were in the middle of expanding the bathroom on the second floor. Megs shook her head. "You're already booked."

"The house is almost finished." Sam glanced at Kelly, who nodded her assent. "The bakery is my first priority now."

"We live in the house, and it would be nice to have a working bathroom." She found that she could smile at that. "Besides, it will be days or weeks before the insurance on the bakery will kick in. I can't rebuild without money." She fingered the business card that she'd stashed in her jeans pocket. Adam was the last person she'd go to for a loan. She didn't care how desperate she got, she would never go to him and beg for money.

CHAPTER TWO

It took two days to get clearance to enter what was left of the Sweetheart. Even then, Megs had to be accompanied by Will Stone, the town's code inspector. And she had to wear a hard hat. She adjusted the heavy thing on her head and stepped over the threshold of her bakery. She stood in what once had been the retail area where her customers bought and ate their pastries. Snow now covered the broken glass of her display cases, the tabletops and chairs. The cash register was buried under more snow and broken timber. She walked through the swinging doors to the kitchen.

The damage here seemed minimal compared to the disaster in the front. Megs walked to the marble top of the work island that had saved her life and ran a hand along it. She glanced behind her to Will.

"The insurance adjuster said he'd arrive at ten. I'm sure he'll be here any minute."

Will nodded and glanced around. "I'm really sorry about what happened, Megs."

"Not your fault." She turned back and wandered to the shelves that still stood connected to the partial back wall. She pulled down a worn but now wet recipe book. She clutched it to her chest. "I'm glad Grammy's not here to see this. It would kill her for sure."

Will cleared his throat, probably not sure what to say to her gallows humor. She shrugged and walked back to the dining area. Being in the kitchen made her wish for something she could never get back.

A tiny man wearing a heavy parka ran into the bakery and glanced around. "Horrible. Simply horrible."

Megs nodded. "Mr. Simon?"

The insurance adjuster brought out his cell phone and started to take pictures. "The devastation."

She glanced around. Yep, that was what it felt like. "But you'll be able to help me rebuild?"

He didn't answer but continued to take

pictures. She followed him around the front room, then through to the kitchen. Will handed him a hard hat, which the man put over his earmuffs. He snapped at least fifty pictures before he glanced at her. "Rebuild? Maybe. Mrs. Sweet's insurance policy covered fire and flooding. But acts of God?" He shrugged. "I'll see what I can do."

"When we spoke on the phone, you assured me that this wouldn't be an issue." She looked around at her ruined business. "I believed you when you said that my policy covered damages."

"Damages? Yes. Rebuilding?" He screwed his face up into a grimace. "Do you realize how much it will cost you to do that? Even on a smaller scale than what you once had?" He shook his head. "Your settlement will help you get started, but I'd suggest consulting a banker for a business loan. You're going to need a lot more than what I can offer."

The image of a certain banker's face popped into her head. No. Never.

She closed her eyes. Why couldn't this ever be easy?

Mr. Simon walked past her and into the

kitchen area. She raised her brows questioningly at Will, who shrugged and followed the insurance adjuster. Maybe she could go into one of the Traverse City banks to get a loan. The bakery had a strong track record of sales, almost a century of them. Surely that would get her the funds she would need. It shouldn't matter that she'd only been in charge of the business for four months, right?

Mr. Simon promised to inform her of the settlement within a few days. She shook his hand and thanked him for being prompt. Will Stone also shook her hand, but he paused before leaving through the front door. "I hate to say it, Megs, but Mr. Simon's right. Anything to do with construction these days costs a lot. The insurance money will help, but you're probably going to need a loan to cover the difference."

She knew that, even as she resisted the idea. But she also knew she would do whatever she needed to avoid having to ask Adam for money. Anyone but him.

She thanked Will again, then locked the door behind him after he left. She sighed and walked back to the kitchen. She needed someone to give her advice. Someone who knew the business and could direct her. Problem was the person she'd depended on wasn't here anymore.

Decision made, she grabbed her purse and locked the door and then walked down the street to where she'd parked her car on Main, since they still weren't allowing vehicles on Lincoln.

She drove out to the countryside cemetery, where four generations of Sweets had been buried, and parked on the side of the road before trudging through the snow up the hill to where Grammy lay buried. She brushed the snow off the headstone marking her grandparents' graves, then stood and clasped her hands in front of her. "I suppose you know why I'm here. The Sweetheart is in trouble, and I don't know what to do."

She paused, listening to see if her dear Grammy would be able to communicate with her from the beyond. But only silence answered her.

Not that she'd expected to actually hear anything.

She thought of Grammy and how she and Pop Pop had kept the bakery going even through the lean times during the Great Depression and the sugar shortages of World War II. They'd rebuilt after a fire had destroyed the kitchen when her father had been a baby. They'd never given up, but had poured their hearts and souls into the Sweetheart.

They'd expect no less from her.

She kissed her glove, then rested it on the headstone. "Thank you both. I won't let you down."

She walked back to her car, determined to make things work. Somehow.

MONDAY MORNINGS REQUIRED enough coffee without a visit from the district manager. Adam sighed and poured himself his third cup, as well as one for Dave Thompson. He took both mugs to his office and handed one to his boss. "I don't remember us having a meeting planned for today."

Dave chuckled. "If I announced every time I was going to visit, I wouldn't find out nearly enough about how things are really running in my branches." He looked out the glass walls to the lobby area where a customer filled out a deposit slip at the stand and another stood at Eva's window making his withdrawal. "Not that busy for a Monday morning, I see."

"The weather has really affected the traffic the past few weeks. Besides, the snow birds are in Florida and won't return until April or May." Adam didn't worry about the trickle of customers in January. But looking at the frown on Dave's face made him rethink that position. "The winter months tend to be slower in Northern Michigan."

Dave huffed and claimed the chair in front of Adam's desk. "I thought when I brought you here that I was getting a go-getter who would make things happen in this area. Not a man who would offer excuses before he'd even started."

"I am a go-getter, but I'm also realistic." Adam rubbed his forehead above his nose where a tension headache threatened to form. He opened his eyes and looked at his boss, who waited for more. He sighed again. "The community had a setback last week when several businesses suffered from snow damage. Many of those business owners are our customers who will be looking to rebuild. I wanted to talk to you about an initiative that will not only leverage the business we have, but bring in more."

Dave nodded. "I'm intrigued. Go on."

Nothing like spitballing and making up things on the fly. Sure, he'd spent time considering options and alternatives for the community since the buildings had collapsed. But he hadn't put anything concrete down on paper. They were merely ideas in his head at the moment. Adam put his hands on the desk in front of him and leaned slightly forward. "When you hired me for this location, the biggest obstacle you explained was the public image of the bank. Foreclosures on homes in the community were at a high. Deposits were down. And the previous bank manager was seen as the villain in the town drama."

"Sounds right."

"In the current crisis situation, I'd like to change the bank's image so that we're seen as a benefactor. Set up a community fund to help those who lost the most. Extend low-interest-rate loans to business owners who'll need to build again. Make the bank a partner with the community in order to improve not only the businesses, but also our image." He sat back in his chair. "If I can change that, I can bring in more money. We will be their first choice rather than last."

Dave took a sip of his coffee then nodded. "Solid ideas. You think you can write up a plan and get it to me by the end of the day?"

Did he have a choice, really? "Absolutely."

Dave stood, so Adam rose to his feet, as well. The other man extended his hand. "I look forward to seeing what you come up with."

They shook hands, then Adam escorted Dave to the door of his office. He opened it to allow the other man to walk through. Dave turned back when he was halfway out the door. "I hope this works. You have ninety days to prove it to me, or I'll have to reassess who I have at the helm of this branch."

"Understood." Adam kept the smile on his face even as the bottom fell out of his stomach. Ninety days? An ambitious plan like his would take almost that long to be put into place. He watched as Dave greeted

Eva, then walked out to his car in the parking lot. He entered the lobby and let himself into the teller's area. He waited until the customer in front of Eva had left before addressing her. "Dave was here."

Eva didn't look at him but nodded. "I saw. Everything okay?"

"Remember those ideas you said were locked in your head?"

"Yep." Eva turned and gave him a smile. "You ready to hear them?"

He nodded and regarded the tiny woman. He'd been told by Dave that she was a dynamo and his biggest ally in the branch. It was time to see if it was true. "I'll buy you lunch, and we can discuss what we both have in mind."

"You're on." She straightened the bills in her drawer so they faced all in the same direction. "And you might want to consider going to the town hall meeting tomorrow night. They're discussing the Lincoln Street situation and what to do."

If he could present some of his ideas to the town council, perhaps he could get their support in helping turn around not just the community but also the bank. He nodded.

"Great idea. Thanks. You're worth every penny we pay you."

She glanced up at him with a smile. "Then, maybe you can send more of that my way?"

He laughed. "In ninety days, if I'm still here, I'll ensure it happens."

MEGS ENTERED THE high school auditorium and scanned the crowd to find her sister. Kelly had promised to get them three seats together for what was sure to be a packed town hall meeting. Already they'd had to change the venue from town council chambers at city hall to the high school when people had called for details about the evening's meeting. And if the half-full room was any indication, they had been correct in switching to a larger space.

Kelly waved at Megs from a spot in the middle of the fifth row. How she had missed her sister when she'd been living in Nashville pursuing her music career. Grammy's death had brought her back, one bright light in those dark days. She walked down the aisle and stopped when she found Adam sitting at the end of the fifth row. He had his dark head bent over a stack of three-by-five note cards and didn't notice her. She'd have to squeeze by his tall, lanky form to get to her sister. She cleared her throat, and he looked up at her, his chocolate-brown eyes peering into her hazels. "Excuse me. I need to get past you."

He didn't seem to understand her English but stared at her. She held up her hands as if to ask him what the problem was. He stood but didn't move into the aisle to let her pass. Instead, she faced a dilemma: squeeze by him with her back to him or turn to face him as she attempted to walk by. She decided she couldn't spend any more time looking at him and turned her back to him to squeeze past. The tight quarters made her brush her arm across his chest. If she'd still been in high school, she might have described the event in her diary and swooned as she told her sister about it. Instead, she ignored the fluttery feeling it brought to her belly and walked toward her sister. She glanced behind her and found Adam watching her. He nodded at her before returning to his seat. Megs rolled her eyes and took the open seat next to Kelly.

Activity on the stage brought Megs's attention to the front of the auditorium. She leaned closer to her sister. "This should be interesting."

Kelly's eyes twinkled. "The meeting or that awkward moment with Adam?"

"You saw that?" Megs groaned. "A gentleman would have stepped out into the aisle to let me pass, but he wouldn't budge. Not that he was ever anything but a cad."

Kelly's eyebrows raised at this. "A cad? Been reading regency romances again with your free time?"

"Free time seems to be all I've had lately since I can't seem to get a loan." She shook her head and glanced at the agenda someone had thrust into her hand. "This is probably just another waste of time."

"Since when has the community coming together to help out ever been a waste? I think the accident has made you cranky." Kelly stood and scanned the rear of the auditorium, probably searching the audience for Sam. "Don't let what's happened change you, Megs. You're better than that."

"You sound like Grammy."

Her sister turned back and nodded. "And

maybe she'd kick your backside until you got out of this funk, too." She paused and waved, then sat down next to her. "Grammy wouldn't give up on the Sweetheart."

"I haven't given up." Megs adjusted her coat around her shoulders since there was a chill in the auditorium. "I'm being realistic. I've applied to two banks for a business loan. Struck out at the first place, and the second wouldn't even take my application because I haven't owned the bakery long enough." She sighed and shook her head. "Worked at the place for fifteen years, but apparently that doesn't mean a thing when you're asking for tens of thousands of dollars."

Kelly nodded toward the end of the aisle. "So talk to Adam."

"Be serious." She glanced at him quickly and then shook her head. "He's the last person I'd go to for this. You remember what he was like in high school."

"*Was* being the key word." She looked up at Sam as he approached them. "Hey, babe."

Sam bent over and kissed her sister's cheek. "Full house tonight." He looked around and nodded at several people. "I would have been here earlier, but my inspection went longer than planned with Will."

Kelly and Megs held their collective breaths. With a soft voice, her sister asked, "And what did he say?"

Sam shrugged. "He approved all the changes." He gave them both a wide smile. "We're officially finished renovating."

Kelly squealed and jumped up to hug him. "All that work and time."

"It was worth it, right?" He let go of Kelly and put an arm around Megs's shoulder. "You girls actually have a beautiful fully remodeled home."

"You mean, you and Kelly do. Grammy left it to the two of you." Megs smiled despite the sour feeling in her belly. "Congratulations, you guys." She joined the group hug and willed herself to feel happy for the couple who seemed to have everything going right for them. Finally.

A gavel sounded on the podium onstage, so they ended their celebration and took their seats. Megs took another glance down the aisle at Adam, who still studied his note cards. She wondered what that was all about.

Rick adjusted the microphone. "Testing. Great. If we could all settle down, we'll get the meeting started. I know there are a lot of questions and concerns about what's been going on. If you didn't receive an agenda for tonight, hold up your hand and I'll make sure you get a copy." He shielded his eyes with one hand as he looked out at them then nodded. "Good. First, let me express my regrets about the loss of property. I'm glad to say that there were no fatalities. Randy Simms remains in stable condition at the hospital, but Vicky tells me she expects to bring him home next week."

Several people clapped at this. Rick joined in for a second or two, then continued. "Next, I'll have our town code inspector Will Stone talk about the damage the businesses on Lincoln received and his expectations of what happens next. Will?"

Will took his place at the microphone. "Thank you, Rick. And like you, I am grateful that there was no loss of life. The businesses, on the other hand, took quite a hit. The hardware store had minimal damage, but the bakery, aquarium, bookstore and the apartment complex have suffered quite badly." For the next several minutes he described what Megs already knew. The shell of the buildings stood, but the interiors had been wiped out. Rebuilding was now the priority for not only the business owners, but the community members, as well. "I know I'm missing my cinnamon roll fix like you are." He looked out into the crowd and smiled at Megs.

She put her head down. Without her hands in dough, her life felt emptier and colder. She longed for the heat of the ovens and the scent of yeast and sugar. She'd tried making cookies and bread at home, but it wasn't the same. She missed the Sweetheart. Her bakery.

"In terms of rebuilding, I'd like to introduce someone who is dedicated to bringing back the Lincoln street businesses. Our local bank manager, Adam Hawkins."

Her jaw dropped. Will had to be mistaken. Adam was dedicated to himself and his own interests alone. Certainly not to Lake Mildred's.

ADAM HADN'T EXPECTED applause as he took the stage, but he hadn't expected stunned silence, either. He shook it off, reminding himself they remembered his past and not his present. He put his note cards on the podium and took a sweeping glance out over the audience. He found hazel eyes staring at him from the fifth row, but chose to ignore her for the moment.

He nodded to Will. "Thank you, Mr. Stone and Mr. Mayor. I appreciate this opportunity to present Foster Community Bank's proposal to rebuild Lincoln Street." He flipped the first card over. "And that's what this is—an opportunity to come together as partners in redeeming what was lost." He glanced out again and squelched the nerves radiating from his fingers, making his note cards tremble. He found Megan staring at him. He kept his focus on her. "Foster Community will offer low-interest-rate loans to those business owners affected by the snowstorms, whether directly or indirectly. After all, what happens to one of us touches the entire community.

"We are also proposing a community fund to raise the funds necessary to help in the rebuilding process. I have set up an account where anyone can donate a dollar, five, ten. Whatever you have. Foster has agreed to match all contributions." He flipped the next card. "We want to be a partner during this difficult time. And I hope that together we can rebuild and revitalize Lincoln Street as well as Lake Mildred. Any questions?"

Hands shot up around the auditorium. He wanted to groan, but Eva had warned him about this. Rick approached the podium and pointed to a gentleman near the front. "Mr. Finney?"

"You said low interest rate. How low?"

Adam smiled. A question he was prepared for. "Three percent less than the current rate, which will save the business owner thousands over the life of the loan. And no application fee or closing costs."

"Why would Foster be willing to work with us now when many of us lost our homes before because they refused?"

A hard question, but again he'd come prepared. "I regret how things were handled in the past. Those responsible are no longer with Foster Community, and we are working hard to repair those bridges we burned. I have been brought here to salvage the relationship the bank once enjoyed with you all. We want to be your source of sound advice and help you achieve your financial goals." He stopped before he sounded anything more like a public-relations brochure.

Another hand, and a familiar guy stood. Adam wanted to ask someone else, anyone else for a question, but he stood and waited.

"And we should believe you why?"

His smile faltered slightly at the sight of his old friend Shane Lee. "I approached the bank president regarding these plans, and she has agreed to them all in writing. I have copies of our proposal should anyone need one."

"I still don't trust a word you say. We all remember what you were when you left here." Shane took his seat.

Adam winced. He'd anticipated that something like this might come up, but he'd hoped it would come from someone else. "I grew up here, so you all know the boy that I was. But I've returned as a changed man. I don't want to see us lose any of the businesses, including the aquarium store.

Let's work this out together. I'll be in my office every day and every hour the bank is open this week and next for those who want to discuss this plan further."

He glanced out at the audience but didn't see any more hands. Most had gone down after the last question, which meant he had to rebuild more than the bank's reputation. He had his own to consider.

AFTER ADAM'S PROPOSAL from Foster Community, there was another rival branch manager who stood to offer assistance. But Megs noted that it didn't come close to what Adam had offered. There was no talk of a community fund with matching contributions. Or lower interest rates.

Maybe Adam had changed. Megs shook her head. She meant the bank had changed. The Sweetheart had been a customer for longer than she'd been alive, so it had been a no-brainer to keep the accounts there as they were before Grammy died. And though she hadn't been affected by the foreclosures, she knew many of her customers who had been. The town's population had shrunk by almost a quarter during that time. Slowly, it was changing for the better. People were now buying homes that had been sitting empty for years and bringing their money to spend in her shop and others.

She stole a glance down the aisle to where Adam sat listening to the other bank manager. Had he changed from the angry bully she remembered? The one who hurt others to keep everyone at a distance? He turned and found her looking at him. She turned back and tried to keep her focus on the speaker, her cheeks heating at getting caught.

After another hour, the session broke up with Rick assuring everyone that there would be a follow-up next week at the town council meeting. Megs rose to her feet and reached behind her to grab her thick coat. The snow had stopped for now, but the frigid temperatures had returned with a vengeance. She struggled to get the parka over her shoulder when a helping hand intervened. She turned and looked up into Adam's long thin face. She stammered and cursed her flaming cheeks. "Thanks."

"I meant what I said up there, Megan.

I'm here to help." He glanced past her, at her sister and Sam, then nodded and left.

Megs turned to Kelly. "What was that about?"

Her sister shrugged. "Sounds as if he wants to help you."

"I don't want his kind of help." But she felt less sure of that than before.

"But you might need him more than what you want."

Megs noticed him walk up the aisle to the back of the auditorium before getting stopped by several people with questions. He leaned down to hear them better and seemed interested in what they had to say. He seemed so different from the boy who had bullied her and her friends. Less hostile, more willing to help. But could she trust him? She already had two strikes against her with the other banks. What could it hurt to try the third at Foster with Adam?

But to help her case, she'd be sure not to show up with empty hands reaching out.

WHEN SHE RETURNED HOME, she scoured Grammy's cookbooks for the best recipe to use for what she had in mind. She needed to tempt Adam with her sweet treats, but it had to be special. Something more would be required than a batch of chocolate-chip cookies if she expected him to hand her a loan for thousands of dollars. It had to require an effort on her part since she was asking for the same thing from him.

Cannolis? She wrinkled her nose. Those always sent the wrong message, especially if it was a gift for the opposite sex.

Strudel? Nah, she didn't want to come across as flaky as the pastry.

She willed Grammy to direct her hands as she flipped through pages, as if the woman could tell her from the other side what to do about the business. The back door opened, and Kelly breezed in, her cheeks flushed and lips swollen. Megs gave a smirk but returned her gaze to the cookbook. "Said good-night to Sam?"

Kelly brought her fingers to her face and nodded. "That man sure can kiss."

"Hmm, I'll have to take your word on that." Despite the fact that she'd known Sam longer and perhaps in some ways better, it was her sister's attention he had snagged. She flipped through more pages and sighed. “So now that you’ve gotten the all-clear on the house, what are you two going to do with it?”

Her sister hung up her bright pink wool pea coat on a peg, then took a seat across the dining room table from her, snatching a cookie from an overflowing plate. “Good question. The will won’t be out of probate for a few more months, so it’s not as if we have to decide right this minute.”

Megs looked up at her. “Do you think you have the money to buy out Sam’s half? Or are you two planning on something more permanent?”

Kelly teased, “Now that I don’t have my paycheck from the bakery, I have even less money than before. And Sam hasn’t mentioned the future lately. Maybe he’s having second thoughts.” She munched on her cookie for a moment before she said, “The best thing would be to sell the place. As much as I hate to say it.”

Megs shook her head. “Sam’s planning a future, all right. And you’re the only one he’s intending to spend it with.”

Kelly shrugged. “I don’t know. Maybe.”

"Definitely."

They both looked around the renovated dining room that now opened into the living room. It would be a shame to have to leave not only their family home, but the beautiful showcase that Kelly and Sam had turned it into. But for them to each get their share of the inheritance, it meant selling would probably be their best option. Kelly frowned. "I don't want to think about that right now. Crazy meeting tonight, huh? So are you going to finally meet with Adam and discuss that loan?"

"That's what I'm working on." She held up the cookbook and pointed to a recipe. "Does he look like a Napoleon kind of person?"

Kelly took the book from her. "He's too tall. You thinking of buttering him up with one of your pastries?"

"I need him to see that I'm more than just doughnuts and cookies. That I've got a head for business as well as baked goods." She picked up Grammy's old recipe ledger that now had a warped cover from the water damage. She opened it and with a finger traced the blurry handwriting. The ink had run on certain pages, and she wanted to howl at the loss of not only the recipes but Grammy's notes. This book was her legacy from the woman who had taught her to cream sugar and sift flour. Her mentor who ate the first piece of her peasant bread and sampled her crème fraîche. She ran a hand down one page. "I keep hoping that something will jump out as the perfect recipe."

"Like this?" Kelly turned the page around of the cookbook she'd been looking at and pointed to their grandmother's handwriting. "She wrote that these were perfect for desperate times."

"I'm not desperate." At her sister's doubtful expression, she shook her head. "I'm not. Worse comes to worst, I take the insurance money and start over somewhere else."

"But then it wouldn't be the Sweetheart."

"It would. Just in a different location." She took the book from her sister. "But it wouldn't hurt to try. Right?"

She read over the recipe for baci, a small Italian cookie that Grammy recommended dipping in chocolate. It looked easy. Simple but elegant. And she had all the ingredients already. It could work.

At this point, it couldn't hurt.

MEGS TOOK THE cream canvas bag from her backseat and carefully placed it over her arm as she shut the door. She glanced up at the bank and took a deep breath to calm the buzzing bees that filled her belly. She could do this. She could go in there and prove to Adam that the Sweetheart deserved that loan. That she could meet the repayment terms without a struggle.

She had to do this.

Another deep breath, and she walked forward. She'd arrived ten minutes before her appointment time, but she hoped that he would see it as a sign of her determination rather than desperation. She opened the front door and allowed Mr. Finney to enter before she followed him inside.

The lobby looked the same as it always did when she brought in the daily deposit, but it felt different today. Ominous. Foreboding? Megs really had to stop reading those regency romance novels for a while. She felt as though she was going off to face the lion in his den, and knowing Adam as she did, it might not be that inaccurate of a description.

She signed in on the clipboard then took a seat to wait her turn, putting the bag at her feet. She glanced inside at the plastic container of baci that rested on top. She'd had Kelly and Sam taste test them before she had filled the container for Adam and his staff. If Kelly's and Sam's moans of pleasure had been any indication, she had something special in her arsenal against the bank manager.

Adam's office door opened, and the man himself stood in the frame. He looked taller, thinner than his high school days, and he wore a tie and suit rather than a letterman's jacket and worn jeans. It was the look in his eyes that made her pause. The wariness remained there.

"Megan Sweet?" He called her name as if he didn't know her. As if he'd never hurt her.

She took another deep breath and rose to her feet. Grabbed the handles of the tote bag and brushed past him into his office, trying to ignore the spicy scent wafting from him that hit her nose as she did so. She took the chair in front of his desk and removed the plastic container from her bag and placed it in her lap. Popping open the top, she let the aroma of chocolate fill the tiny office. She removed a napkin with the Sweetheart logo and placed a baci on it before putting it in front of Adam.

He frowned. “What’s this? A bribe already?”

He claimed he’d changed, but he’d just proved that nothing had. He still used words to hurt and belittle. She bristled in her chair and pointed at the pastry. “It’s a treat for you and your staff from the Sweetheart.”

He eyed it, then took it in his hand. She watched as he lifted to his mouth and raised one eyebrow. He chewed it slowly, his tongue darting out of his mouth to lick any crumbs left on his lips. He nodded. “Good.”

“This is just a sample of what I can do.” She brought out her recipe ledger and spread it open. “My grandmother not only left me the bakery, but all her time-tested recipes guaranteed to make the Sweetheart a success for years to come. And success means money, which means you and I both profit. See this recipe for True Love's torte? It's a hot seller especially around Valentine's Day, which is just around the corner and..."

Adam held a hand up. "Recipes and products that sell are good." He paused. "For you, that is. They don't mean a thing to me or the bank."

Megs sat back in her seat and crossed her legs at the ankles. She regretted having worn her practical boots rather than the high heels that Kelly had suggested. "Sex sells," her sister had told her as she pulled out a different outfit from what she currently wore. Maybe she should have worn the low V-neck wrap dress rather than the turtleneck sweater under the wool blazer.

"So that's it? You're turning me down already?" She rose to her feet and grasped the handles of the tote bag.

Adam came around the desk and put a hand on her shoulder. "Where are you going? We're just getting started."

"I'm not about to sit here and let you mock me. I put up with enough of that when we were teenagers." She grabbed her coat that she'd draped on the back of the chair. "I have too much to do to waste my time with you."

Adam left her side and stood in front of the door. "You're so quick to judge me."

"You taught me well."

They glared at each other until he blinked. "I'm not mocking you, Megan. I'm trying to tell you what I'm looking to get from you. While I appreciate you bringing the cookies today, I need more than that to risk the bank's money on the bakery." He seemed to rise several inches as he gestured to the chair she'd vacated. "Now, why don't we sit down and go over what I need?"

She eyed him warily. She didn't have much choice, did she?

ADAM BLINKED SEVERAL times before Megan took her seat and placed her coat and bag in the empty chair next to hers. He let out the breath he realized he'd been holding and returned to his seat behind the desk. He pulled out a folder and handed it across to her. She looked up at him with those hazel brown eyes filled with past pain. He knew he'd been responsible of putting that there and had regretted it every day since. "If you look at the first page in your packet, you'll notice that we will need several documents from you to support your loan application. Tax returns. Profit and loss statements. An accounting of all your assets and liabilities."

She looked over the list and seemed to grow pale in front of him. He'd heard a lot about her prowess as a baker, but very little about her as a businesswoman. Perhaps she hadn't had to worry about the business side of things until recently. He was tempted to reach out and put a hand over hers. Instead, he clasped his hands in front of him and rested them on the desk. "It sounds a lot worse than it is. Your accountant will have most, if not all, of these documents. I will try to make this as easy on you as possible."

She peered up at him. "Why?"

"Because I want to help you out."

"Again, why?"

He cleared his throat. "Listen. I know our past history doesn't make us friends or anything, but I could be your ally." Before she could ask again, he barreled on. "Because

I want to make up for what happened. Because you didn't deserve anything I did to you. Or your friend."

She paused and eyed him again. "If we work together on this loan, I want a couple of ground rules."

That didn't sound good. "Okay. Like what?"

She held up one finger. "No talking about the past. Especially about Kenny." Two fingers. "Nothing to be done or offered out of pity or trying to redeem yourself because of said past." Three fingers. "And we keep this on a purely professional level."

"I can agree to those terms. Should we shake on it?" He held his hand out to her.

She stared at it, but kept her hand to herself. "And no touching."

"You have a lot of rules." He gave her a smile, hoping to lighten the mood. But the scowl on her face remained, so he put his hand back on the desk. "Fine. No touching."

She looked back at the document list. "I have some of these items with me. Jack thought I should be prepared for anything."

She reached into her bag and pulled out a thick binder. “I’m glad I listened to him.”

Was this Jack her boyfriend? He tried to recall anyone with that name in their graduating class but couldn’t come up with a face. And why did the thought of Megan with a boyfriend make his heart sink? Not that she shouldn’t have one, as pretty and as sweet as she was. But the idea didn’t settle well with him.

She flipped through the binder and unsnapped the rings so that she could remove several pages. She handed them across the desk to him, and he stood. “I’ll go make some copies of this for your file. Can I get you anything while I’m out? Coffee? Water?”

“Hot tea, if you have it.” She flipped through the binder some more, then pulled out two more pages. “You may need these, as well.”

So civil. So polite. Adam nodded and took the pages as well as the cookies to the break room with him. He found Eva having her lunch, and held out the container. “Megan Sweet brought treats for the entire staff.”

She chose one and bit into it, closing her eyes as she chewed. "That girl is truly talented." She opened her eyes and looked at him. "Lord knows I loved Addy, but her granddaughter is even better at making the bakery run than she was."

Adam leaned against the counter and crossed his arms over his chest. "You think the Sweetheart would be a good risk?"

Eva finished swallowing her bite and smiled. "Don't you?"

"I've got to make copies." He held up the pages and walked out of the break room. Why was he already second-guessing Megs's request for a loan? It wasn't as if he was using his position to repay her for the past by green-lighting the request. Besides, she probably still had that same backbone that had helped her stand up to him and would use it again to rebuild the business and make it thrive.

He got his copies and returned to his office, handing Megs the originals. She spent several minutes reorganizing the pages back into her binder, and placed it in her bag. She studied the lone piece of paper left in front of her. "I noticed that the document list asks for a business plan."

He sat behind his desk and steepled his fingers in front of his mouth. "Did you come prepared for that, as well?"

"You want it in writing? Rather than me telling you that I sell bread and cookies to the town?" She shook her head. "Because that's my plan for the business. Not that difficult to figure out."

He frowned at her. "No, I want a written description of your business, your target consumer as well as a forecast for any future growth. How many employees you have and your labor costs. A budget. I want hard numbers based on the information you gave me here." He lifted the pages from his desk and waved them in her direction. "A concrete business plan for the Sweetheart." When she continued to stare at him, he longed to groan. Instead, he put the papers back down. "You do have one, right?"

She stared at her hands. "Only in my head."

"That's a great start, Megan." He watched her until she raised her head to meet his eyes. "If you'd like, I can help you formulate one to go along with your application."

She stood and grabbed her coat and bag. "No, I think I can figure it out on my own. I don't need you to do anything but put in the application." She nodded at him then turned to leave.

He rose to his feet and walked behind her out of the office. "I'll expect your application soon, then."

She didn't say anything but waved at his tellers before leaving the bank.

Well, that didn't go too badly.

MEGS WALKED TO her car and opened the back door to put her tote bag in before letting herself into the driver's seat. *Don't cry. Not here. Leave the parking lot and then you can lose it.* She started the car and paused for a moment before putting it in gear.

Once out of the parking lot, she let the tears that had been threatening since walking into Adam's office fall down her cheeks and drip off her chin unhindered. The fact that she'd had to go to him of all people with hat in hand to ask for money. Then for him to make her feel smaller than an ant because she didn't have a written business plan. And if she didn't have Jack for an accountant, she wouldn't know the first thing about his list of required documents.

She felt like a fool in more than one way. A fool to assume she had the business sense to run the bakery. If anything, she learned that she still had more to find out. And she felt foolish to imagine she could face him again without feeling like a fifteen-year-old afraid of the big bully. Without remembering Kenny and what it had cost him.

Her cell phone buzzed, and she answered it through the speaker phone on her car.

"How did it go?" Kelly, of course.

"I'm not sure exactly. He needs a written business plan, and I don't know the first thing about writing one."

"So we'll Google it and put one together."

"And the application is like twenty pages long." She sniffed. "And it's Adam Hawkins. I don't exactly have the best history with him."

"A lot can change in twelve years."

She was probably right. Megs was glad

she'd made that rule about not bringing up the past. Why rehash it?

Then, why hang on to it?

Okay, her conscience had a good point. Adam seemed to have gotten past all of that, and she needed to, as well. *Just bury those memories away. Let it go. Move on.* And every other cliché she could think of. "Yup. It's for the best. Time to forget and—"

Her sister chuckled. "I didn't say forget. I mean, he was a bully who hurt a lot of people. But he seems to have changed, so that's all over with." There was a pause. "Right?"

It was over, all right. Because there was no way that Megs was going to let him humiliate and hurt her or anyone she loved ever again. "Right, Kel." Her phone buzzed, and she checked the caller ID on her car's console. "That's Mom. I'll be home in about ten minutes."

She switched the call using the buttons on her steering wheel and took several deep breaths. Talking to her mother was easier now that they had established a relationship as adults, but she couldn't forget the abandonment. “Hi, Mom. Where are you today?”

Her mom chuckled. “Megs, I’m not exactly a globe trotter. Still in Florida, though Stan is talking about moving on to Arizona where it’s drier. Better for his asthma.”

Megs frowned. “Stan? I thought you were with Michael.”

“His kids didn’t like me much, so there you are.” Her mom was suddenly silent on the other end. “Listen, sweetie, I heard about the Sweetheart. Are you going to be okay?”

How? Lake Mildred, Michigan, was a long ways from Florida, but obviously the local grapevine extended that far south. “I’ll be fine. I met with the bank manager to discuss getting a loan to rebuild the bakery.”

“Can you afford that?”

“I can’t afford not to.” Because the option of doing nothing was unthinkable. “Unless you have some money you could lend me.”

Her mom laughed, but it sounded false. “Oh, sure. Let me send you a check for twenty thousand. Will that work?” Another pause. “You know if I had anything, I’d be the first to be sure you had enough.”

Her mom had never been one she could depend on in a crisis. She’d always turned to her dad, then Grammy after he’d died. They’d been the steady, strong ones in her life. Not her mother. “Thanks anyway, Mom.” Megs turned down the street where she lived. “I’m almost home, so I’ve got to go. Have fun with Stan.”

“Oh, I will.” Then her mother was gone.

Megs ended the call by pressing a button and gripped the steering wheel. It was time to start depending on herself. Time to do something different. Be something different. She could be strong on her own. Do it all herself.

But first, she’d have to research what a written business plan required.

CHAPTER THREE

THE LIGHTS FROM the cabin lit the way for Megs and Kelly as they walked carefully over the icy path, balancing several boxes of pastries and cookies as well as two loaves of sourdough bread. Kelly glanced behind them. "I'll get our overnight bags after we put all this inside."

Megs kept her eyes forward, skirting around a patch of ice. "Why we have to hold this girls' weekend at a remote log cabin is beyond me. Why not a spa or the casino? Just because Jack has the room for all of us under one roof..."

"I think this will be fun." Kelly giggled and walked faster to the front door. "How many did you say will be here?"

"Depends. Every year is different." She paused before the top box could slide off the two others and land in the snow. "I doubt Suzy will be here since she has the baby. And sometimes people bring friends and… Maybe ten?"

They had finally reached the front door. Megs used her foot to knock since her hands were full. "Open up or none of you get any treats."

A woman in a hoodie and sweatpants answered the door. She turned and yelled into the cabin, "Dessert is here. The fun can begin." She took two boxes off Megs's load and held the door open for them. "Penny is setting up all the food in Jack's kitchen. Megs, you know the way."

"Thanks, Shelby." Megs stepped inside the cabin. The front room was a large open space connected to the kitchen and boasted huge windows that looked out into the woods surrounding it. She led the way to the kitchen and smiled at Penny, a friend since high school. "Hey, you made it this year."

The older woman shrugged. "My husband decided that he could live without me for a weekend." She gave a smile, but it didn't quite reach her eyes. "Tell me you brought those chocolate things I love."

Kelly set her load on the countertop. "If

they've got chocolate, then yes she made them. She's been baking all week for this."

Penny opened a lid and took out a mini éclair and bit into it. "You're a genius, Megs. Honestly."

If only she could convince Adam of that. She still had the application sitting on top of her dresser, waiting for her to work on that. And the business plan. She should have been doing that rather than baking for the girls' only weekend. But she had priorities. She looked around the room. "Where is everyone?"

"I found some old photos in the study and they're having a look at those. There will be cries of laughter any minute now, Jack wasn't the cutest of babies." Penny's brother lent them the cabin for their girls' weekend every year despite his sister's constant teasing. Penny smirked. "Those pictures probably won't help get him married off any time soon, I'm afraid."

Kelly's eyes lit up, and she left to join the other women. Megs chuckled. "So didn't need to know that about my accountant."

Penny shrugged and continued getting the food set up for their first evening. Megs reached for a container and stacked crackers on a plate. "Everything okay? You look a little pale."

"Nothing this weekend won't help." She started to clear her throat and turned away from the food. "Sorry. Smoker's cough."

"I thought you gave that up."

"It comes and goes. Right now, it's my nasty habit." She turned and looked at Kelly, who had brought in their overnight bags. "You warn your sister about this weekend?"

Megs raised one eyebrow. "And ruin my fun? I don't think so."

Penny laughed then started to cough again. "I really gotta quit for good this time."

Megs put her hand on her friend's arm, then walked into the living area where a fire had been lit in the wood-burning stove. The mulled wine was already in the pot on top of the stove. She took the wooden spoon resting on a shelf above and gave the wine and fruit a stir. The front door opened, and she greeted Lizzie Allyn. "You're off work for the weekend?"

"Didn't want to not participate in the shenanigans again." She pulled her wheeled suitcase inside and placed it near the pile with the others. "Did I miss anything?"

"Just baby pictures of Jack."

Penny and Shelby had started the girls-only weekend a few years ago. And each year, the festivities got bigger and louder. Friday night was mulled wine and catching up with everyone. Saturday meant hiking with canteens of wine, a huge dinner, then a pajama fashion show and board games. Sunday was a big brunch after sleeping in late. Megs rarely took a weekend off from the bakery, but it was always this one. She wouldn't dare miss the party.

Kelly walked back into the living room. "Here's a picture of Rick, our now illustrious mayor, with Jack mooning the cheerleaders." She chuckled. "I forgot about that. It's amazing what the years can do to your memories."

"I was there, and trust me, I'd rather forget it." Penny carried the platter of cheese and crackers into the living room and placed it on the coffee table. "Seems we're all here if we want to get this party started."

Shelby returned to the living room followed by Lizzie, Suzy, Page, Tori and Presley. "Now that roll call's been taken, I'm starving. Is it all ready?"

"Yes, no thanks to you." Penny brought over a tray of mugs and balanced it on the seat of a chair from the dining room. "Would someone like to serve the wine?"

Since she was standing near the stove, Megs did the honors of ladling the hot spiced wine into the mugs and distributing them to each woman. All but Lizzie. "I can't."

Conversations stopped as the group turned toward her. Suzy asked what they were all thinking. "Why, Mrs. Allyn, are you pregnant?"

Lizzie's cheeks colored. "I wish. We've been trying, but nothing's happened. I'm off alcohol and caffeine to boost our chances." She got up from the sofa and walked into the kitchen to get a bottle of water from the fridge. She turned back to find them watching her. "It's no big deal."

Suzy put her mug down. "We don't have to drink this weekend if it would make you feel uncomfortable."

Lizzie waved her hand at her. "No, don't

abstain on my account. I'm fine." She took a seat on the sofa. "Well, not completely fine. I mean, I'm failing as a woman since I can't even get pregnant."

Page, ever the counselor, shook her head, her long blond curls moving in waves as she did so. "A woman's sole purpose is not to have a baby, Liz. You shouldn't accept that as a failure on your part."

"It feels like it, though." She raised her head, tears glistening in her eyes. "But Rick's been great. He's trying so hard to cheer me up." She gave a soft smile. "He even surprised me one night by wearing my pink teddy to bed."

Shelby covered her eyes. "Don't want that image in my head."

"He only did it to get me to laugh. And it worked. Especially when he couldn't get out of it, and I had to cut the thing off him."

The women chortled and sipped their wine. Penny looked around at the other women. "Matt and I…lost another baby this past October." She put a hand on her flat belly. "My problem isn't getting pregnant, but staying so. My ob-gyn doesn't know why the miscarriages keep happening."

Shelby reached over and put a hand over her sister's. "I had a feeling something was wrong. Why didn't you tell me?"

The sisters shared a glance. "Matt and I had agreed not to tell anyone until I was past the three-month point. I couldn't tell you."

"Well, Mom figured it out." Shelby rushed on before her sister could reply. "She didn't say anything to anyone but me, so no one but those of us here know."

Megs leaned in close to Kelly. "That's one of the rules this weekend. Whatever is shared between us stays here. Consequences of sharing our secrets is pretty stiff, too."

Kelly nodded and glanced around at the other women. "I want to thank you for including me this weekend. Megs has told me about her wild weekends before, but I'm glad to be a part of it this year."

"Me, too." Presley, a tall redhead, lifted her mug. "Thank you for the invite."

Suzy put her arm around her friend and squeezed. "I had to include both you and Page this year. You're my besties."

"How's Will surviving with little Ben on his own?" Page asked.

Suzy shrugged. "His mom's staying with him over the weekend, so he's not exactly alone. And as they say, not my circus, not my monkeys."

"Plus he's watching my twins, don't forget," said Tori. "So he's going to have his hands full. But my brother was a marine. He'll be fine." Tori saluted her sister-in-law with her mug. "I need more wine. There seems to be a hole in this cup. It's empty already."

She rose from her seated position on the floor and went to the stove and held up the ladle. "Anyone else?"

Kelly joined her and got her mug refilled. Megs stared down into hers. This weekend seemed to be starting on a negative note. She got to her feet and joined them at the stove for a refill. More wine would be good.

Shelby cleared her throat. "Okay, I have some good news. I'll be finishing my associate's degree in business management this May." She gave a short laugh. "A two-year degree that's only taken me four to finish."

"That's great news!" Tori took her seat on the floor again. "Does that mean your boss, Walt, will give you a raise now? You've been managing his cottage and rental property business for a while."

"Which is why getting my degree has taken four years." Shelby shrugged. "We haven't talked about it, but when he comes back this spring from Florida I'll really need to nail him down about my future there."

"Walt's getting up in years. You might want to talk to him about taking over the cottages when he retires." Penny shrugged when her sister stared at her. "What? You've talked about that before. I'm only saying it out loud."

"He has a grandson with a fancy degree to inherit them."

"A grandson who hasn't been back to Michigan in how many years? While you've been putting in your own blood and sweat into this place. More than any of the Austins, so why not ask for what's due to you?" Penny sipped her wine.

"It's an idea." Shelby took a napkin from

the stack on the coffee table and filled it with several rounds of cheese and crackers. "Who else has news?" She turned to Megs. "What are you going to do about the bakery?"

The one topic she'd been hoping to avoid. Megs sipped her wine rather than answering. Kelly leaned in as if to share gossip. "She went to the bank this past week and talked to Adam about getting a business loan to rebuild."

"That man is seriously hot." Page fanned herself. "And I heard he's single."

"He can stay that way for all I care." Megs rose to her feet and walked into the kitchen to grab the box of mini éclairs and cream puffs. She pulled out a plastic plate and put the empty box to the side before taking the pastries into the living room. "We all remember what he was like in high school."

Presley raised her hand. "Not all of us grew up here, so no, I don't." She glanced at Page. "And you were in the next town over."

Page shrugged and picked a cream puff. "I still heard stories about him, though."

She glanced at Megs. “A real heartbreaker with the ladies.”

Megs bristled. “And a big bully to boot. He took delight in hurting those weaker than him.” She loaded her napkin with mini éclairs. “I’d rather not talk about him if that’s okay.”

“I sense a story there.” Presley looked to Kelly who shook her head. “But you don’t have to talk about him if you don’t want to.”

“I have some good news.” Kelly glanced at all of them then smiled widely. “Sam called me to say that a couple of the songs we wrote together sold and will be on Tyler Wilson’s next album.” Everyone hooted and cheered.

Her sister, the songwriter. Megs grinned. Who would have thought? Kelly the singer, sure. But she hadn’t known her sister had the writing talent until she’d sung a song she’d cowritten with Sam last November. “And that’s only the beginning for you both.”

“Any wedding bells ringing for you two yet?”

Kelly blushed but shrugged at Penny. “Who knows? We have to sort out what’s going to happen to Grammy's house. Do we sell it or not? Brandy said we have time before the real estate season really starts, but we need to make some decisions. And soon."

"Where is Brandy, by the way?" Suzy glanced at Lizzie. "I thought you invited her."

"I did, but she called this morning and said she wasn't feeling well."

Suzy nodded. "The flu is getting around. Half of my patients have it and pass on their germs to the other half. It's a never-ending cycle."

Tori stood and lifted her mug. "Ladies, here's to good health and hanging on to it."

They all clinked their mugs and settled in to devouring the pastries and finishing off the mulled wine.

THE MORNING LIGHT peeked in through the slats of the vertical blinds that covered the large picture window in the living room. Megs took her top pillow and placed it over her face. Way too early to be thinking about getting up after a night of drinking many mugs of mulled wine. She rolled over to find Shelby percolating coffee using an ancient kettle on top of the wood-burning stove. Another tradition.

Megs sat up and gave a long yawn while stretching her arms up and out. Might as well get the doughnuts and strudel ready for the morning meal. She stacked her pillows next to Shelby's in the corner and folded her blankets beside them. "How long have you been up?"

Shelby shrugged. "Couldn't sleep. I've been stuck on what Penny said about asking Walt to run the cottage business." She glanced at Megs. "Think I could do it?"

"You've been working there since you were fifteen. If anyone knows that business, it's you." She walked into the kitchen and rinsed off a tray before placing a paper towel over it. She started to stack doughnuts on it. "It's like the Sweetheart. It's all I know."

"So what are you going to do about the bakery?"

"Kelly was right. I'm applying for a loan, but Adam asked for a written business plan and I don't know the first thing about that."

"Hey, I could help you with that. No

problem." Shelby reached over and snagged a honey cruller. "That's part of what I learned for my degree. Do you have time next week?"

"Time is all I have at the moment. Thanks." Megs claimed one of the stools at the kitchen island and helped herself to a sour-cream doughnut. "Then maybe Adam will get off my back with this loan app."

"You doing okay working with Adam?"

Megs made a face. "I guess. I mean, I told him that we couldn't discuss the past. And absolutely no touching."

"And he agreed just like that?"

He had, which puzzled her. The old Adam would have argued with her nonstop until he'd gotten whatever he wanted. Instead, the new Adam had gone along with her proposal.

As if he didn't care.

"Just like that." It had been too easy. He had to have some other kind of angle he was working on with her. Because he never did anything at face value. He always had a scheme going. "He doesn't matter."

"If you say so."

More of the women started to stir, so

Megs busied herself slicing the raspberry strudel that she'd made yesterday. She handed a slice on a napkin to Lizzie and a cup of herbal tea. "Thanks."

"My Grammy had a recipe she called the baby maker. I'll see if I can find it if you want to try it."

Lizzie gave her a half smile. "I might take you up on that." Penny clapped her hands. "I filled the canteens with wine, so once we're dressed, we can go on our hike."

Kelly whispered to Megs, "Hiking with wine? I don't get it."

"It's not just a hike to the lake," Megs explained. "We do a polar-bear plunge before we run back. The wine is to give us the courage to go out naked into the icy water."

Kelly's head snapped up. "Skinny-dipping in February? Isn't the lake frozen over?"

"Not completely." Megs shrugged. "You don't have to if you're chicken. Not everyone does it." She winked at her sister then joined the others to get ready.

"I WANT TO see the man in charge!" The old man stood in the middle of the bank, hands on his hips. "They said he has money, and I need some."

Adam saved his work on the computer then walked into the lobby. "I'm the branch manager. Why don't you step into my office and we can discuss what you need?"

The man pushed Adam aside and took a seat in one of the chairs. He whistled as he took in the furnishings of the office. "No wonder this bank never has any money. You spend it all on decorating."

Adam took a seat across from him and folded his hands on the desk in front of him. "Mr. Taber, right? You used to drive the school bus."

The old man eyed him and gave a short nod. "For thirty-eight years, I picked you kids up and dropped you off. I'm retired from there now, but I work part-time at the hardware store." He paused. "Or I did until that roof collapsed."

"When do they expect the hardware store will reopen?"

"Few weeks, best they can tell." Mr. Taber shook his head. "Problem is, I live on social security and that job. How can I pay my bills if I'm not working?"

Adam pulled out a pad of paper and started to take notes. "That's a very good point, Mr. Taber. How much did you usually make at the store?"

"In a week? About one-fifty after taxes." Mr. Taber shifted in his chair. "I wouldn't normally complain, but that paid for groceries and gas in my car. No paycheck means I'm not eating."

Adam wrote all of this down, then pulled out a withdrawal slip from a desk drawer. "Will three hundred dollars help you in the meantime?"

Mr. Taber's eyes narrowed. "And what's the catch? I done told you I'm not working, so I can't pay it back."

"We set up the community fund to help people like you survive until the hardware store reopens. And we don't expect to get paid back." Adam signed the slip. "Will tens and twenties be sufficient?"

The old man nodded. "Fine."

Adam stood and left the office. He went up to one of his teller's windows and waited as she ran the transaction and counted back the money. Adam placed it in an envelope and took it with him to his office where he held it out to Mr. Taber. “You’ll let me know if you need any more.”

Mr. Taber stared at the envelope. “Is this some kind of joke? I walk in with empty hands and walk out with cash? Maybe that’s why you people never have any money.”

“This all comes from donations, Mr. Taber.” He thrust the envelope in the man’s hand. “People want to help others like yourself in this community.”

“I never took no charity, but I appreciate the help.” He stuffed the cash in his coat pocket. “Now, are you done with me? Or can I get out of your hair?”

Adam shook his hand then saw him to the front door. He turned to find some of the other customers watching him. A woman approached him. “How do I donate to the community fund? Can I just write a check?”

Adam ushered her into his office. Sometimes you gave, but other times you received.

BEING A NEW MOM, Suzy had stayed behind to keep the wood-burning stove fed and roaring when they returned from their hike to the lake. She grinned at their wet heads. "You all did it?"

Kelly scowled at her sister and moved closer to the stove to warm up. Megs grabbed the wool blanket that she'd brought with her and draped it over her sister's shoulders. "You've officially been initiated into the girls' club."

"Only had to freeze my nether regions to do it, too." She grasped the ends of the blanket and pulled it around her.

Tori put her arm around her waist. "The only thing is that you can't tell anyone about it. Otherwise, I'm sure we'd get a few spectators."

"Jack." Penny and Shelby nodded at each other. "If he only knew what we did in his cabin each year."

Presley and Page joined Kelly near the fire while the veterans compared notes to years past. Suzy walked up to Megs and handed her her cell phone. "You got a call while you were out there."

"Thanks." Megs checked her caller ID and frowned at the unfamiliar phone number. She pressed Redial.

A male voice answered on the other end. "Megan? It's Adam."

She glanced at the other women, then walked quickly down the hallway to Jack's study. She closed the door behind her. "Is something wrong?"

"I haven't heard from you since we met on Thursday. I'd hoped to have your application so we can get moving on that loan."

Right. The loan app. "I'm not home this weekend. It's going to be the middle of next week before I have it ready for you." Silence on the other end. She sighed. "I'm working on that business plan you asked for."

"If you need assistance, I'd be glad..."

"No." She winced at her tone and dropped her volume. "I mean, no, thank you. I've got someone who's volunteered to help me."

"Good."

A moment of silence while Megs wondered why he'd call her on a Saturday morning. And how had he gotten her cell phone number? Probably from the listing on her personal account. She cleared her throat. "So I need to get back to my friends."

"Sure. Have a good weekend, Megan."

She hung up before she could tell him to do the same.

AT TWO, ADAM helped the tellers get their cash drawers back into the vault and shut the door, spinning the dials to secure it for the weekend. He'd hoped that by being in the office on the weekend, he'd get more traffic from the Lincoln Street business owners needing loans. He'd had one customer besides Mr. Taber. John Striker, who ran the hardware store. The damage had been minimal to his store, but enough to need some assistance.

He tried not to take the absence of the other business owners personally, but it looked as though his efforts to improve the relationship of the bank to the community had a long way to go. He walked his staff out to their cars after he'd locked the bank, then used his key fob to unlock the doors to his truck. He had his hand on the door handle, but he didn't want to go home to an empty apartment just yet. He locked the truck again and decided to head toward downtown and the diner. Maybe a burger and fries would improve his mood.

He entered Rick's diner and saw the mayor leaning on the counter as he chatted with a guy on one of the stools. Adam took a seat several stools down from him and perused a menu, even though he'd already made up his mind what to eat. Rick walked down the counter and put a glass of ice water in front of him. "Haven't seen you in here since high school."

"There's a time for everything." He put the menu down. "I'll get the cheeseburger platter with a diet pop."

"Good man." Rick wrote the order down on a pad, then took Adam's menu and placed it back on the stack near the register. "I'll go put that in for you."

Adam noted the other man at the counter. He had longish dark hair and a beard, but he looked familiar from his high school days. The name rested on the tip of his tongue, but it eluded him. Rick set a plastic opaque cup in front of him with his drink. He followed Adam's gaze. "Jack Novakowski. I believe he was in your year at Lake Mildred High."

Adam gave a short nod. He remembered Jack now. He'd been the kind of nerd that he'd once been fond of ridiculing. But the years appeared to have been good to him. The glasses were gone, and he looked more rugged than his skinny high school self. Tougher.

Adam swallowed hard. He couldn't escape his past no matter where he went in this town. He turned and took a sip of his drink. Motion beside him showed that Jack had scooted down to the stool next to him. He held out his hand. "Nice to see you again, Adam."

Adam hesitated for a moment, then shook Jack's hand. "I wasn't sure if you'd remember me. Or if it was a good thing if you did."

Jack shrugged. "High school is over." He nudged Adam in the ribs. "Good thing, too. What a nightmare, right?"

"They were hardly my best years." They hadn't even been his mediocre years. They'd been horrible, filled with anger and hate. He'd acted out by picking on those who were weaker in the hopes of making himself stronger but had found just the opposite to be true. Didn't matter if they feared him, he still felt like a loser. "I'm glad to say I've turned my life around since then."

"That's the point of life, isn't it? Making yourself into a better version?" Jack took a French fry and dragged it through ketchup. "I heard what you and Foster Community are doing to help the town out. Including our Megs."

He couldn't escape that woman, either. He shouldn't have called her, but he'd been concerned when he hadn't heard back from her about the loan application. And ever since he'd talked to her, she'd been all he'd thought about. "You're the accountant. She mentioned that you'd help her put her loan application together."

"Anything you need, let me know. That woman is a brilliant baker, but she's not as sure of herself on the numbers. But then, she didn't have to be until Mrs. Sweet died in fall." Jack paused as Rick brought out Adam's lunch. "I was just telling Adam that he needs to help out Megs and the bakery."

Rick agreed. "The town isn't the same without the Sweetheart. And I don't mean that I'm just missing my morning bear claw."

"I'm working with her to get what she needs." He put ketchup on his cheeseburger, then squirted some next to his French fries. He did the same with the mustard. He looked up at both men. "I'm serious about helping the community rebuild. There's nothing more important to me right now."

"Good." Rick glanced around the diner. "There's a lot of people like you in Lake Mildred. Neighbors coming out to help each other. I don't think we've had to face a crisis like this in the past decade or so."

Jack nodded. "Rick and I were discussing the bank's proposal to match whatever's donated to the community fund and how we could maximize those efforts. Maybe a fund-raiser to add to the pot. Would you be interested in helping?"

A fund-raiser? He didn't know the first thing about what it took to pull off one of those. But helping? "Whatever I can do."

Jack punched Rick in the arm. "What did I tell you? Now we just need a plan."

Rick rubbed his upper lip, deep in thought. "I have some ideas on this, but I have to wait until my Lizzie is back in town before I can say anything."

"Your wife is out of town? So is Megs." That seemed too big of a coincidence.

Jack laughed. "They're all out at my cabin this weekend for their girls-only annual event. I have no idea what goes on, but I always return to the place being cleaner than how I left it. So who am I to refuse?"

"Maybe we should have a guys-only weekend some time." Rick turned to Adam. "Would you be in?"

"Sure." It wouldn't hurt to have some friends in the community. If Jack could forgive and forget their past, maybe others would, too. "Sounds good."

"Or a Super Bowl party at my cabin." Jack held his hands up as if surrendering and pushed his empty plate away from him. "I've got that beautiful big-screen TV and plenty of chips and beer."

"But they don't deliver pizza out to where you live." Rick picked up the empty plate and left them at the counter.

"So bring it with you before you drive out there," Jack called after him. To Adam he said, "There's a group of us playing basketball tonight at the high school gym if you'd like to join us."

"Trying to get me involved, I see."

"People can't change their opinion of you if you don't show up and prove them wrong. Think about it." He picked up his bill and waved at Rick before leaving to pay at the register. "See you at seven."

Rick returned to the counter and slid Adam's bill near his plate. "You should come out and join us."

"I'll think about it."

"Do more than think, Adam."

After he left the diner, he strolled back to his truck still in the bank's parking lot. He started the engine, but didn't back out of his parking spot. Instead, he debated what to do next. Something Jack had said kept flipping over in his mind. If he wasn't seen, didn't make an attempt to reconnect, then people wouldn't know he'd changed. He thought of two people no longer in his life that should know that he had become a better man. Determined on his path, he left the bank and drove to the old neighborhood.

He pulled his truck into the driveway

then peered at the green-sided house with black shutters. The house he'd grown up in, the one where his parents still lived.

He turned off the engine and sat for a moment, trying to work up the courage to get out this time. He hadn't seen his parents since his dad had told him that he was no longer his son and sent him to military school. He occasionally got a phone call from his mother, usually around Christmas, but Adam figured she hadn't told his dad about it.

He opened the door and got out of the truck. He hoped that his parents would still be home, getting ready to leave for his aunt's house like they had every Saturday night. He wanted to be able to see them for a moment, but have an excuse to leave quickly. He walked up the sidewalk to the front door and knocked on it. The curtain in the window fluttered then the front door opened.

Adam swallowed. "Mom."

"Oh, my. I heard you were back and hoped I'd see you. I look for you every time I go to the grocery store." She opened her arms and he bent down to hug her, breathing in her scent. She still smelled like menthol cigarettes and the familiar perfume from his childhood.

"Winnie, who's at the door?" his father roared from another room.

His mom let go of him and shook her head. "You shouldn't be here."

"I came to see you." He glanced behind her. "Both of you."

His dad looked older, but was still tall and wiry, though he seemed to stoop a little more than before. "What do you want?"

"He said he came here to see us."

"I asked him. Not you." His dad stepped forward and pushed his mother away from the door, putting his arms out to bar Adam's entrance. "You're not welcome here."

"It's been twelve years, Dad."

"It's Mr. Hawkins to you."

His mom tugged on his dad's arm. "Give him a chance, Rodney."

His father turned and held up a hand as if to smack her. She stepped back and bowed her head. So things hadn't changed there, either. Adam's hands tightened into fists. "I came here to see how you both were doing."

"You've seen. Now you can go."

"Sir, I wanted to let you know I've made something of my life. That I'm not the same out-of-control boy who stole your car." He pulled out his business card and held it out to his dad. "I'm living back here now and was made the bank manager at the Foster Community branch in town."

His dad stared at the card, but didn't take it. "We don't bank there."

"I know." He glimpsed over at his mom. "I thought that maybe we could let the past be over. That we could try to repair our relationship."

"You thought wrong. You were always a no-good brat who thought you were better than everyone else. Well, being a high and mighty banker don't make you a thing. A zebra can't change his stripes, and you're still worthless. Ain't worth my time."

His dad spat on the ground, and Adam backed away so that it wouldn't hit his shoes. He put the business card back in his coat pocket. "I figured that it would be pointless to try, but I had to take the chance." He glanced at his mom. "Love you." Then he turned away promptly and walked toward the truck, not daring to look back.

SUNDAY AFTERNOON ARRIVED too soon, but Megs felt grateful to go home. Over the course of the weekend, she'd slept little and drank a lot. The thought of a long nap before dinner tempted her as she pulled her car into the driveway and parked next to Sam's pickup. She nudged her sister, who'd fallen asleep on the drive home from the cabin. "Hey, we're here."

Kelly roused then stretched, yawning widely. "I'm going to collapse on the couch when we get inside. I don't think I have the energy to go upstairs to my bedroom."

"Sounds good." Megs got out of the car and retrieved her pillows and overnight bag from the backseat before slamming shut the door. "I'm going to need some rest if I'm to get that loan application finished."

"You don't want to procrastinate on that thing." Kelly stopped in midyawn when she looked up and saw Sam walking down the stairs from his apartment above the garage. "Hey, babe. We both got home in one piece."

"Good thing." He walked to her sister and kissed her soundly on the mouth.

"Don't ever leave me that long again. I missed you so much."

"I missed you, too." She smiled wider as he took her pillow and bag from her arms and walked to the side door of the house. "You wouldn't believe what I did this weekend."

Megs cleared her throat. "And you won't find out since we're not sharing anything that happened, right, Kelly?"

"Right."

Sam held the door open for them both to enter first. "I'll have to die from curiosity instead."

"Exactly." Megs walked past Sam into the house and winced when Kelly squealed and turned to face them.

The kitchen was full of red helium balloons. Kelly ran into Sam's arms and hugged him. "You remembered."

Megs frowned until Sam explained, "Third month anniversary."

"Right." She moved past the couple and into the hallway that led to the stairs up to her room. She loved her sister and Sam, but sometimes she didn't care for them as a couple. Not that they weren't cute. But they could be a bit much. Especially when she felt so lonely.

Inside her bedroom, she put her pillows on the bed and the overnight bag on the floor. Then fell onto the bed, arms outstretched. A knock on her door made her turn over. Kelly popped her head in. “Sam’s asked me out to dinner in Traverse City. Are you going to be okay on your own?”

“Go. Have a good time.”

“We can bring you something back if you’d like.”

Megs shook her head. “Don’t worry. I’ll be fine. I’ll scrounge up something downstairs if I get hungry later.”

Kelly smiled and looked down at her sweatshirt and jeans. “I’m going to shower and change. So much for my nap.”

“A night out with Sam will be worth it.”

“Yes, it will. Thanks, Megs. I’ll shut your door so you can rest.”

After Kelly left her room, Megs rolled on her back and stared at her ceiling. There had been a time when she hadn’t wanted a relationship, but these days she found herself missing it more. Especially as more in her social circle started pairing up and getting married. She figured it was only a matter of time before her sister and Sam got engaged and kept the house, effectively forcing Megs to move out. Not that it wasn't something that was long overdue.

So many changes in so little time. Grammy dying. Kelly returning. And then her and Sam getting together. And now the bakery destroyed and waiting to be rebuilt.

She sat up and glanced over at the loan app resting on her dresser. It wasn't just the business plan that was keeping her from doing this. And if she was honest, it wasn't the possibility of working with Adam that had stopped her from moving forward. Her problem was her own fear.

Fear that she was making the wrong choice. Fear of letting Grammy down. Fear that the new bakery wouldn't be able to perform like the old one had.

She rose off the bed and walked to the dresser. Picked up the application and looked it over and then at the alarm clock. It wasn't even five yet. With Kelly out of the house for the evening, she'd be able to focus on completing it before she met with Shelby the following night to work on the business plan. And with those two pieces together, she'd be ready to charge forward on the loan and redoing the bakery.

Because that was all she had.

CHAPTER FOUR

ADAM STROLLED INTO the bank on Tuesday morning with a coffee in one hand and his brown bag lunch in the other. He'd had a meeting with Dave at the district office in Traverse City that morning, so he arrived later than his usual time. His boss was pleased with the preliminary results for the first week with the community fund, though Adam had left Dave's office with a reminder that he still had a deadline to meet.

Adam waved to his tellers as he entered, then paused when he saw Megs sitting in the lobby. Had she made an appointment with him that he'd forgotten? He doubted it. He'd certainly remember her.

He walked up to her and waited for her to look up at him. "Did we have a scheduled meeting this morning?"

She blinked several times, then shook

her head slowly. Today she wore a yellow sweater that brought out the golden tones of her hair and eyes. He swallowed, then lifted his bagged lunch. "Let me get this in the fridge, then we can talk. My office door is open if you'd like to meet me there."

She nodded and turned to retrieve her purse and coat. Adam detoured by the teller stand where Eva worked on night deposits. "How long has Ms. Sweet been waiting for me?"

"She was here when we opened the doors." Eva looked over at her. "I explained you had a morning meeting, but she insisted on waiting for you. We offered her something to drink while she waited."

"Thanks." He glanced behind him and saw that she'd set herself up in his office. He hoped that this meant she had completed what he needed for her loan application. "Any other messages?"

"Town council meeting is tomorrow night. You ready?"

Adam gave her a smile. He'd spent most of the previous evening polishing a second presentation of the community fund and emphasizing Foster's desire to establish a relationship between the bank and town. "Can you hold my calls while I'm with Ms. Sweet?"

"Yes, boss." Eva saluted him then smirked. "Important client?"

"They all are." He left her and went to the break room to hang his coat and put his lunch away. He walked down to the restroom to check his appearance in the mirror. Pushed back a strand of hair that had fallen out of its gelled position. Loosened his tie a little so that he wouldn't look so stiff. Took a deep breath. Leaned on the sink and stared at his reflection. *I can do this. I can go in there and help Megan Sweet. Maybe make it up to her for all the horrible things I did to her in the past.*

He rubbed his left shoulder, remembering Kenny and the way she'd stood up for her friend against Adam. The fire in her eyes when she'd warned him to back off. He'd admired her for doing that, the only one who had ever stood up to his bullying. And he'd rewarded her days later by kissing her hard, hoping to bruise her soft lips. She'd slapped him after, but the damage had been done. He had so many regrets.

He left the restroom and strode down the hall to his office. *Let's get this over with.*

She sat in the same chair she had the week before, her legs crossed and hands folded and resting on top of the folder he'd given her. He took a seat behind his desk. "I would have been here this morning if I'd known you were coming in."

"I should have called first." She lifted the folder from her lap and handed it to him across the desk. "All the information you requested is in there."

He nodded and accepted the folder, flipping it open and reviewing each page. He could sense her fidgeting while he examined the figures she'd provided as well as the mission statement for her business. He smiled at her words: "To provide baked goods that fed not only the body, but the soul." A lofty goal.

He put the pages back down and looked over at her. "Everything's good. Thank you for getting this to me in a timely manner."

Ugh. His words sounded stuffy but polite. As if he was keeping himself at a distance from her. But then she'd set up the groundwork for that herself.

She nodded and rose to her feet. "Is there anything else you need from me?"

Forgiveness.

He only wished for that. Had worked so hard to get it from his other victims by starting with an apology and seeing if he could make up for his past. To redeem his once worthless life into one that would make his parents proud again. Not that it seemed as though anything he did would ever cause that to happen. "Yes, I'll need to interview you regarding some things that go beyond what's in the application." He glanced at his watch. "Do you have the time to do that now?"

She sat back down. "What kind of interview?"

He put his hand on the folder. "What's in here is part of the picture I need to paint to my loan officer to approve your request. But I've found that sometimes there are things that the application doesn't cover. Especially in your case when the request is for money to rebuild."

"Fine. What do you want to know?"

He opened a desk drawer and withdrew a yellow pad of paper and pen. "Is it all right with you if I take notes during our conversation?" When she nodded, he wrote her name at the top of the page and underlined it several times. "How much of a loan were you looking for?"

She shrugged. "I don't know. How much are you offering me?"

"You don't have a ballpark figure in mind?"

She reached up and rubbed the space between her eyebrows. "The insurance company is offering a little over half of what I need to rebuild what I had before. So I'm estimating about another twenty-five thousand dollars would work." She looked up at him. "But I'll take more if you're offering it."

He wrote the figure down. "The proceeds of the loan would cover what expenses?"

"Materials for the reconstruction as well as what my contractor will charge me for his labor." She pointed to the folder. "I wrote that in my application inside."

"We're painting a picture, remember?" He made some further notes. "Close your eyes." When she frowned at him, he shrugged.

"Humor me. Please." She closed her eyes. "Picture the perfect bakery that you want to build. See it? The display cases. The tables and chairs. In the kitchen, picture the ovens and industrial mixers. Now open your eyes. What did you see?"

"Two sets of double ovens. My old marble worktable. Stainless-steel triple sink. And a dishwasher that actually works." She bit her lip and thought for a moment. "Tall tables with stools in the dining area. Glass display cases with a tall refrigerated case for take-home-and-bake items."

He nodded and wrote down the words as she spoke them. "Sounds like a nice place."

"It is. And it's completely different from what I used to have." She shook her head and stood. Grabbed her coat and purse. "I don't think I can do this right now."

Adam frowned at the pad of paper. "But things were going so well. What's wrong?"

"What I just saw in my head wasn't what I expected. I'm sorry. Things have changed." She put her coat on and zipped it up the front. "I'll make an appointment for tomorrow."

She started to leave but he walked over

and reached out to grab her coat sleeve. She turned and looked down at his hand, then glared at him. "I said no touching."

He removed his hand and held it up. "Please don't leave. This process is almost done, and I can get your application over to my loan officer within the hour. Don't walk out on your future, Megan."

"That's the problem. I didn't plan on the future I just saw." Her shoulders slumped slightly then she put her purse down in the far seat and removed her coat. "Fine. But I'm not committed to what I just told you, right?"

"Why wouldn't you want it to be?" He took his seat once more as she did the same. "So it wasn't what you expected. Is that so wrong?"

She took several deep breaths. "Sam's been working on floor plans similar to what the Sweetheart was before. He thought that was what I wanted."

"But you don't?"

She frowned. "That perfect bakery in my head? It's different than the original. I didn't realize it until just now."

"Then, I'd say we did some good work,

wouldn't you?" He smiled over at her and almost cheered when she returned it for a brief moment. "When are you looking to receive the proceeds from the loan?"

She wrinkled her nose. "Last week?" She chuckled. "I'll be getting the insurance check within the week to get the work started, but I'm looking at a construction schedule over the next six to eight weeks."

He made that note, then looked up at her. "That's all I need for now. I can call you if something else comes up? Once I get this over to my loan consultant, I should hear something within the next forty-eight hours." She nodded but didn't move to leave. They sat in silence for a long moment until he sighed. "Today was nice. I'm sorry for being such a jerk to you back in high school."

"Rule number one, we don't talk about the past."

"I know the rules, but we need to talk about the elephant in the room if we're going to work together." He leaned across the desk. "About that day with Kenny..."

"I can't talk about him." She got to her feet and put her coat on. "You agreed to the rules from the beginning, yet you broke two of them today."

"You live by a lot of rules, don't you?"

She flipped her hair out from beneath her coat. "I'm a baker who follows the directions on a recipe to get a superior product. What are directions if not rules?" She retrieved her purse and turned back to look at him. "If the recipe for us working together means following those rules to get the best result, then that's what we have to do."

She made sense, as much as he hated to admit it. "Okay. No touching. No talking about the past." Her eyebrows rose until he added, "Nothing done for pity or to redeem our past. Keep it professional." He paused. "Was that it?"

"You may think I need you, but I don't."

He watched her walk out of the bank with her head held high, a reminder of the girl she'd been. He looked down at the application and his notes. He might have agreed to her rules, but there was one he had to break. No matter what, he was going to get this loan for her to make up for what he'd done to her.

MEGS CLEARED OFF the dining room table so that Sam could go over his construction plans for the new Sweetheart. Kelly smiled and put her arm around his shoulders. "I can't wait to see what you came up with. Aren't you excited, Megs?"

After her meeting with Adam and her vision of the perfect bakery, she wasn't sure. "None of this is etched in stone, right? We can change things as we need to?"

"You're the boss. It's whatever you want it to be, Megs." He set up the laptop so that the sisters could get the best view. "Within the constraints of the physical structure and the budget, of course."

Kelly rolled her eyes. "And don't be talking about upgrading the hot-water heater or reinforcing the foundation." She turned to Megs. "He gets his mind set on mundane details sometimes."

"If we do an inspection and discover it needs to be done..."

"You love spending money on details that the customer isn't going to see or care about."

"They're going to care if they fall through

the floor or if Megs needs hot water and can't get any out of the faucet."

Megs held up her hands in a timeout pattern. "Are we talking about the bakery or are you rehashing an old argument?"

"Fair enough." Kelly sat on a chair next to her sister. "But I'm serious. Watch out for him."

She squelched a grin and took a deep breath. "Go for it, Sam. We're ready to see what you came up with."

Sam pressed a few keys on the computer and the old bakery facade came on screen. Megs winced. She was afraid that Sam might be right about needing to reinforce the structure that was already there. He pressed another key, and it faded to a rendering of what the new bakery could look like. The front window with the original script Sweetheart surrounded by red hearts. But the front door was now wider with two French doors. "Are those practical for my business?"

Sam shrugged. "It was just an idea I've been floating around. And so is this." He pressed more keys, and the old dining room flashed on screen then faded to a replica of the new. It had the same tables and chairs, but the L-shaped display cases had been replaced by two straight line cases with the register in between. Gone was the swinging door into the back kitchen. Instead, it was left open with a clear view from the front of the bakery to the double ovens.

Megs stood and leaned into the computer to get a better view. She glanced up at Sam. "An open concept?"

"I thought people might like to watch you while you work. You're an artist in the kitchen." He pressed a few more keys. "But I also did a plan with the old swinging doors."

Kelly nodded. "I like that one better."

"Of course you do. It looks like it used to be." Megs stood and crossed her arms over her chest. "I'd consider a more open look, but would I feel as though I was on display along with the pastries? I don't know."

"Like I said, these are just ideas to give us a starting point."

He pressed more keys and brought up a picture of the old kitchen, which faded to the new, improved rendering. She noted the double ovens and wished she could have seen a double set of them. Four ovens would mean she could bake more products at the same time, cutting down how long she spent in the kitchen. She'd have to see if there was room in the budget for that.

"And this is the upstairs loft for you."

He'd created a studio apartment above the bakery for her. She smiled at his thoughtfulness. If he was planning on marrying Kelly, then he would want her to be moved out before he could move in. She could see where his mind was. "I like the loft."

She glanced over at Kelly who watched Sam with a soft expression on her face. "You used my idea."

He reached out and brushed aside the bangs from her face. "It was a good one."

Megs cleared her throat. "How much would this cost me?"

Sam gave her several sheets with figures. "The top page there is if we go cheap. Spend more on what the customer sees." He glanced at Kelly. "But the second shows if we spend more to upgrade the kitchen."

"What would it cost to get two sets of double ovens? Would that fit in my budget?" She flipped through the pages and paled at the figures listed. "And how much do you need to hire workers to get this done before Easter?"

"Besides Kelly, maybe two more guys, and I can get this done before then." He watched her as she read the proposal over. "And if you want to get a proposal from another builder, I'll understand."

"Why would I do that? I know you and your work." She handed him back the pages. "Of course, all of this depends on how my loan app goes."

Kelly touched her arm. "Do you think it went well?"

It had, for the most part. Adam had seemed different. Mature. She could even admit that he seemed friendly and eager to work with her. Until he'd brought up high school. If they could keep it impersonal yet professional, it would be fine. But if he insisted on recalling things that were better left alone, she wasn't sure. She wanted to forget the horrible past rather than reliving it by seeing him. And then, when he'd touched her… It had felt like a lightning bolt up her arm into her chest. But in a good way. "I guess. I'll hear something by Thursday."

"I don't know how you'll be able to sleep until then."

Megs wasn't sure, either. If she couldn't get the loan, then rebuilding the existing place was out. She'd have to relocate, and that was definitely not in her plans. "We'll hope for the best but prepare for the worst."

"You're so calm. I envy that." Kelly reached out and rubbed her shoulder. "What's your reaction to Sam's designs?"

"They've definitely given me something to consider." She glanced at her sister. "I don't know if I want things to be exactly as they were. Would you be okay with that?"

Kelly shrugged, but didn't look Megs in the eye. "Why wouldn't I be? It's your bakery, not mine." She pointed at the renovated dining room they were standing in. "I didn't consult with you on the changes we made here, to the house, so I wouldn't expect you to do the same on this."

"But I do want to consider it, your opinion, I mean." She stared at the laptop that was still scrolling through Sam's ideas like a slideshow. "I'm not sure about how open

I want it to be. And I'd hoped to have room for events like Suzy's baby shower we did last fall." She shrugged. "I guess there's still time for me to do some research."

"Check out Pinterest. Tons of design ideas there that might help you."

"Thanks." Megs looked over at Sam, who returned to the dining room with a cup of coffee. "And thank you, too. This was more than I expected."

Kelly put her arms around Sam's middle and looked up at him, love shining in her eyes. "He's amazing, isn't he?"

Megs swallowed and tried to squelch the finger of jealousy that crawled up from her belly. What would it be like to have a good man in her life? To gaze adoringly at someone who was on her side and made her feel confident, as if anything were possible?

Adam's face flashed in her mind for a moment. But she wised up and shook it off.

THE CHECK FROM the insurance company arrived in the mail, so Megs drove into town to get that deposited into her account as soon as she could. That meant work could start on the new bakery. She walked through the lobby and found that she was the only customer there. She moved to Eva's station and handed her the check and deposit slip she'd filled out at home. "Payday came a little early this week."

Eva accepted them and ran them through her machine. She leaned in and dropped the volume of her voice. "Has Adam called you about your loan yet?"

Megs shook her head. "No, has he heard something?"

"He's been on the phone most of the day, so I'd hoped he had good news about your application."

She turned and glanced behind her toward the wall of glass that separated Adam's office from the lobby. Sure enough, he was on the phone, and by the looks of things, the conversation was not going well. She'd hate to be on the other end of that call if his thunderous expression was any indication. "I'm sure I'll hear about it soon enough." She turned back and accepted her receipt from Eva. "I'm meeting Sam at the bakery now to see what we can salvage from the damage."

Eva patted her hand. "Good luck with that, sweetie. We're all pulling for you."

Megs gave her a nod, then turned to leave. She met Adam's gaze through the window, and he waved her over. Maybe he did have some good news. She walked to his office, and he stretched the phone cord to get up and open the door for her. He indicated a chair, so she took a seat and waited, unzipping her coat in case it was going to take a while for him to finish his conversation.

Adam bit out his words. "I'll get back to you on this, but understand that I am not happy. Nor will my client be when she hears this."

Dread hit her in the belly, and she squeezed her hands together. Was he talking about her? She waited for him to hang up the phone, knowing his words before he said them. "That was the loan consultant. Again. She has some concerns about your application."

Megs closed her eyes and willed her lunch to stay down. "Concerns?"

"The bakery's ownership is transferring over from your grandmother to you, but the will giving you the business is still in probate?"

He raised his eyes to hers, but she knew that he already knew the answer to that. She gave a short nod. "Zac believes everything should be wrapped up within the next few weeks. Maybe a month, since everything was spelled out clearly and there's been no objections. Is that a problem?"

"Not for me." He scowled at the phone as if it was to blame. "The consultant seems to believe it's a bigger issue than it is." He returned his gaze to Megs. "I'm fighting her on this, and I already have a call in to the district manager to get his approval."

"Worst case, what does this mean? No loan?"

Adam shook his head. "More like the approval would wait until the will has cleared probate and ownership passes legally to you." He leaned back in his chair and rubbed his eyes. "But I'm not going to make you hang around that long. You need the bakery up and running now rather than later."

Yes, she did. She needed to get back to work. To feel purpose in her life again. "Do you think you'll be able to get approval for my loan or am I wasting my time here?"

"It's not a waste of time at all. But this is why the bank got the reputation it did. We were slow to act when people needed us." He adjusted the things on his desk. "What I'm about to say is going to sound like I'm breaking one of your rules, but I'm sincere about this." He looked up at her. "I intend to help you. No matter what I have to do or whose head I have to go above, I'll make sure you get what you need."

"Because you feel sorry for me?"

"Hell, no. You're too strong for that. It's because you're on the right side of things, and I'm hoping my superiors will recognize this." He got up from his chair and came to sit on the edge of the desk nearest her. "You're a good business risk. Your bakery has a strong record of sales as well as a long history with us. Even if your name wasn't at the top of the company masthead before now, you are responsible for that. Don't let this setback take anything away from you. And that's all this is, a setback. This isn't over."

Moisture gathered in her eyes, but she

refused to cry in front of him. He believed in her. Even after all this time and all their history, he knew she could make this work. And if her enemy could believe that, then why couldn't she? She gave a short nod. "It's only the beginning."

He smiled and winked at her. "That's my girl."

CHAPTER FIVE

ADAM SLAMMED THE phone down, then rose to his feet. He wanted to get out of here. Needed to flee from the bureaucracy and the lack of common sense. The clock on his computer said it was well past lunchtime. He opened the door to his office and stalked out into the lobby. His assistant manager, Stacey, looked up from her desk. "Something wrong?"

"Nothing a walk in the cold won't cure. I'm taking my lunch. Be back in thirty minutes." He walked down the hall to retrieve his coat from the break room. He thrust his arms through and buttoned up the long woolen trench coat. Stuffed his hands into gloves and shoved the knitted cap over his head. He stalked back through the lobby and out the door to the winter air. He took a deep breath of icy oxygen and smiled. Ah, that was more like it.

He started walking down the sidewalk toward the middle of town and ended up passing the diner and the department store, Roxy's. He kept moving until he reached the entrance to Lincoln, which was still barricaded to automotive traffic. He squeezed past the wooden slats and surveyed the damage the snow had left. There was movement on the far end of the block by the hardware store, where damage had been more minimal, while the apartment building had been torn down, unable to be saved or rebuilt without costing more money than starting over fresh. The bakery and the aquarium looked empty still. He went over to stand in front of both businesses. One he was trying to help; the other had refused it. He walked closer and used his hand to shield the light to see if he could see anyone inside the aquarium shop. He noted movement toward the back and knocked on the front window.

The movement in the back stilled, but a man started walking toward the front door. He paused a moment before he unlocked it and stuck his head out. "We're closed."

"Shane, I want to help you."

"Like you helped Megan Sweet?" Shane gave a bitter laugh. "Word on the street is that you can't even get a successful business like the bakery to get approved for a loan. How in the world do you expect to help me?"

Adam groaned at the thought of his bad day leaking out into town gossip. But he wasn't going to give up on Megan, so he certainly wasn't going to abandon Shane. "Come to my office and let's talk. Discuss options. See what I can offer you."

Shane shook his head. "I don't need your help."

"Then, talk to my other banker if you can't work with me. Don't be so stubborn that you miss out on a chance to get your business back."

"I've already got an offer from another bank, but thanks."

He started to shut the door, but Adam stuck his foot between the door and the frame so he couldn't. "What terms are they giving you?"

"None of your business."

"Let me see if we can get you better."

He pulled out his business card and held it out to Shane. "I've heard you're a shrewd businessman, so do the smart thing and discover if Foster can sweeten your deal."

Shane took the business card but then dropped it on the ground before pushing Adam out and slamming the door shut. Great. Another gold star for an already stellar day. He picked up the business card from the ground and wedged it between the door and the frame.

THE DEBRIS FROM the roof collapse had finally been cleared, and Megs surveyed the damage it had left behind. She had the money from the insurance company, but she couldn't depend on the proceeds from a loan at this point to get her to where she wanted to be. It was time to figure out what she could save.

She pulled two chairs from where they'd been pushed aside to get the larger pieces of the structure out. While the tables and chairs had survived the damage, the display case windows had shattered and couldn't be replaced cheaper than it would be to buy new. Or in Megs's case, new to her. She'd been in contact with a retailer who had some used ones on sale that would fit into her budget.

Sam brought out a hard hat and plunked it on her head. "Safety first." He put his hands on his hips and looked around the space. "It's not as bad as it could have been. Some elbow grease needed, but you could get everything back in shape again."

Megs shot him a look and moved around to walk into the kitchen. She ran her hand on the marble-topped worktable that had saved her life. After a little cleaning, maybe she could use it again. The ovens had been crushed in the disaster, however, so they would need replacing, too. The walk-in cooler needed to be repaired, but she'd have to weigh the cost of repair versus replacement on that, as well. She slowed and gripped the nearest counter. "Where to begin?"

Sam put his hand on her shoulder. "I realize things aren't going the way you want, but it will work out okay in the end."

"I'm having a hard time believing that right now." She picked up a whisk that cowered under the worktable. "If I can't get the loan..."

"We'll make do." He cleared off a spot on the worktable and pulled the laptop from his messenger bag. "I've been tweaking the original plans to accommodate a smaller budget just in case." He pulled up several images. "This way we use as much as what's here rather than trying to start over from scratch." He pointed to several pictures. "I can make things work, but the biggest expense, of course, will be rebuilding the roof."

They both looked up at the gaping hole that showed the gray clouds overhead. She took a deep breath. "Well, I have some good news on that front. The building owner's insurance company will cover most of that. He will bill me for my share of the remainder. Still, it's going to be in the thousands."

"Any word on when that construction will happen?"

She shrugged. "They've started on the end by the hardware store, but should be down on my end by the middle of next week barring any more inclement weather."

"Good." Sam nodded and pressed more

computer keys. "What would you think about moving what we can save into storage temporarily? I've been researching some facilities, and I found one not far from here with available spaces."

"Why are you doing all this for me?"

"We're practically family, so why not? Besides, you're my next building project, so I have a vested interest in what you decide."

"Kelly said that Shane next door approached you about working on his place, too."

"He did. I told him that you hired me first, but I think I can help him out, as well. Especially if I hire a crew. There are quite a few people looking for jobs now in this town. And being right next to each other, I could supervise both work sites."

"Can I afford a crew?"

He looked down at her. "You can't afford not to have a crew. The longer you stay closed, the more it's going to cost you in the long run."

"I know, I know." She looked around the barren kitchen. It had once been infused with life. Warmth from the ovens. Scents of yeast and sugar floating in the air. Now it was cold and empty. "Okay, yes to all of it. The storage unit. The crew. Whatever you need. Because I have to get back to baking. I'm feeling a little lost without the Sweetheart."

"I'll get right on it."

There was a knock on the front door. Frowning, Megs walked out to the dining area and opened the front door to find Adam. "Something wrong?"

He cupped his hands and blew on them. "It's cold out. Can I come in, please?"

"It's not as if it's any warmer in here, but you're welcome to enter."

She held the door open for him, and he stepped inside. Shivering, he made a face. "You're right. It's not any warmer." He looked up at the absent ceiling through the hole in the roof. "This doesn't look very good, does it?"

"Did you have a reason for stopping by?" He was starting to irritate her. Not that it took much for him to get her to that point.

He nodded toward Sam, then turned back to her. "I was able to get a preliminary approval of your loan."

Oh, thank goodness for that. It felt as

though a burden lifted off her shoulders. "Thank you, Adam. I know how hard you worked on that for me."

"That's the good news."

That didn't sound very promising. "And the bad?" He again glanced at Sam. Megs waved her hands. "He's family so whatever you need to say, go ahead."

"There're certain conditions they want met first. And I should warn you that they're not going to be easy." He paused and closed his eyes, pinching the bridge of his nose. "Basically it's hoops they want you to jump through to get final approval."

"What kind of hoops?" Hopefully, they'd be ones that she could manage.

He opened his eyes and looked at her. "They want you to have a reserve fund of about half the requested loan. A cosigner who has collateral. And a shorter repayment plan than normal."

Her heart fell at each item he listed. She didn't have a thousand dollars in savings, much less over ten thousand. And the only person she could approach to cosign was her sister, who was in the same position she was with the probate. And how much shorter of a term? "All of this because the business is still in probate? Is that normal practice?"

"They're erring on the conservative side. But I'm still working on them. These conditions are ludicrous, and I should be able to eliminate most of them, if not all."

Couldn't she have one thing work out for her? That was all she was asking. "I'll have to see what I can do."

Adam tried to give her a smile, but it waned almost as soon as it appeared. "I'll keep you updated." He looked around her bakery. "We'll get you back in business somehow. I promise."

Megs walked him to the door and let him out before turning back to face Sam. "So what do I do now? They're asking for a lot."

"I might be able to help you with some of that."

Megs insisted, "No, you're doing enough already. I can't ask you to give more than what you are."

"Hey, like you said, I'm family. And that's what big brothers do. We help out our little sisters." He pulled her into a hug. "We'll figure this out, kid."

Megs rested her cheek on the front of his vinyl parka. She closed her eyes and soaked up his strength to face whatever lay ahead.

THE TOWN COUNCIL chamber was packed, but less people had shown up than at the meeting held the previous week in the school gymnasium. Adam took a seat in the middle, since he wasn't planning on speaking unless called upon. He was here to support the community more than anything else. He draped his wool coat over the back of his seat, then turned to look around the room to see any familiar faces. He thought his dad might show up, but he didn't see his familiar face. He noted that Shane Lee stood across the room from him in the middle of a group. He'd hoped that he'd see Shane at the bank before now, but he couldn't force the man to accept his help.

Rick banged the gavel at his seated position at the C-shaped table on the platform. He leaned into the microphone. "We'll be starting in another minute. The signup sheet to speak is located at the podium on my left."

"Adam." He turned to find the town inspector calling his name. He stood and held out his hand and shook Will's. "Have you had many people come see you at the bank?"

"Some," he replied. "I'd hoped to see more, to be honest." He scanned the room. "I guess the negative feelings in the community are stronger than I had originally anticipated."

Will patted him on the back. "Give them time. That, and patience. I've learned that in my job."

"They need to rebuild now. How long are they going to wait? Until the spring thaw? They're losing money while they stay closed." He shook his head. "Sorry. I'm letting my frustrations out on you, and you have nothing to do with it."

Will considered this, then pulled out a business card. "Call me if you need a sounding board. I might have some insight for you."

"Thanks." Adam pocketed the card, then took his seat as Rick called the meeting to order.

Unlike the previous town meeting, the Lincoln Street situation wasn't the only topic. There was other town business that had to be taken care of first. But when Lincoln was brought up, most people seemed to sit straighter in their seats. Including Adam. It had stayed upmost in everyone's minds.

Rick took the microphone from one of the council members. "An update on events since last week's meeting. Rebuilding has begun on many businesses, but the street is still barricaded from traffic until further notice. The community fund at Foster Community bank has a current balance of about twelve hundred dollars before matching funds. Which is good, but not great. That is why I am proposing that a fund-raiser be held to get a bigger balance in there. This is a fund that will help out those affected by the destruction. It can cover things like giving money to those who aren't working since their business isn't open. It will pay for food, rent, heat. The diner has a donation bucket on the counter, but I'd like to see someone spearhead a bigger event." He shielded his eyes and glanced out into the audience. "I thought I saw Adam Hawkins out there."

No, not him. He was out of his league

on that front. He slipped a little in his seat even as people turned to look at him. Rick nodded. "What do you say, Adam?" When Adam didn't respond, Rick held up a hand. "I know I put you on the spot, so we'll talk after this." He shielded his eyes once more. "And I know I saw Megan Sweet squeeze in before we started. If I could talk to the two of you after the meeting, we might be able to jump-start this unless someone else wants to volunteer."

Silence. Adam shuddered. He felt as though he'd been called down to the principal's office. Which was a familiar feeling, since it had happened to him often during middle and high school.

The meeting ended, and Adam considered leaving before Rick could corner him and convince him to run the fund-raiser. But he was out of luck since the mayor rushed up to him as Adam put his coat on. "I had hoped to talk to you before the meeting, but didn't get a chance. And you said you were willing to do what was needed to help. I figured that since you were in charge of the community fund, you'd be perfect for being on the fund-raising committee."

A committee. This made Adam a little less tense. "Nothing like being put on the spot. I think I'd be able to work with a committee, though."

"Good." He and the mayor shook hands, then both men turned to look at Megan. She wore a yellow sweater that made her golden even under the fluorescent lights. "I'm hoping you'll work with Adam on this, Megan?"

"I appreciate the offer, Rick, but I have to worry about getting the bakery rebuilt, not raising money." Someone waved at her, and she waved back.

"You're planning on doing the repairs yourself?" When Megan shook her head, Rick gave a smile. "Perfect. Then, you'll have time to plan this while you're waiting for the bakery to be finished."

"I don't..."

"I want someone on the committee who's been directly affected by this catastrophe. And you're better equipped to work on this than Harry or Shane or any of the others since you helped your grandmother in the past." He gave a half shrug. "No offense to either of them."

Adam glanced at Megan. "I don't think she's comfortable working with me on the committee. I can bow out."

"No, I want you in on this, as well." He shuffled his papers, tucking them inside a knapsack. "You both have the most vested interest in seeing that this fund-raiser is done right. I'm depending on you both."

And then he left. Adam looked over at Megan. "If you'd rather quit..."

She raised her head at this to glare at him. "I don't quit."

"Neither do I." He looked around the council chambers. "I guess that means we're stuck with each other on this thing."

She didn't say anything and stomped away. Adam glanced over at Rick who was now in conversation with Will Stone. He narrowed his eyes at the mayor. Why the two of them? His logic was sound, but he believed there was more going on to this request that they work together on the fund-raiser. Well, it didn't matter. He'd raise money to help the community. And in the process, if it improved the bank's image, it was a win-win situation for everyone.

MEGS TOOK OUT the cookie sheet of red-velvet crinkle cookies and sniffed appreciatively. If the smell was any indication, these would be fabulous. Especially once they were cooled and topped with the cream-cheese frosting. She used the spatula to remove the cookies from the sheet and place them on the racks to cool.

A knock on the front door. She glanced up at the clock and noted that it was after noon already. Where had the day gone? She'd spent time at the library browsing through the cookbooks, then come home to pore through the cookbooks she'd checked out to find new recipes, one of which now cooled. She wasn't expecting anyone, but she put the cookie sheet on the counter, then dusted her hands off before walking from the kitchen to the front door. She peered out and sighed. Adam.

He turned as she opened the door. So tall that the top of his head almost reached the top of the door frame. He gave her a smile, but she didn't return it. Instead, she leaned on the door. “Did we have an appointment?”

He ducked his head and entered the home. “No, but I was driving by and spotted your house. I was hoping you had some time to talk.” He glanced around. “Is this a good time?”

“I’m working back here. Follow me.” She ushered him into the kitchen so she could finish taking the cookies from the oven. She didn’t care that the kitchen looked as if she hadn’t done dishes in a week. She’d been working that morning, and he wasn’t going to judge her for that.

Adam pointed at the cookies on the cooling racks and licked his lips. “I’ve never seen red cookies before.”

“They’re a new recipe I’m trying.” She nodded to the stools at the work island. “Take a seat, and I’ll frost some for you when I’m done.” She put the remainder of the cookies on the cooling rack, then retrieved the frosting from the refrigerator. She found a knife in the silverware drawer, then frosted three cookies and retrieved a small dish to place them on. She handed Adam the plate. “Coffee?”

He nodded as he took his first bite. Then moaned loudly. “These are fabulous. What do you call them?”

“Frosted red-velvet crinkles.” She poured him a cup of coffee from the carafe then retrieved the powdered creamer and sugar from Kelly’s stash. “I thought they might be good for Valentine’s Day if I dye the frosting pink.”

He frowned at her. “That’s only a few days away. You won’t be open by then.”

“For next year. I’m always looking for ideas. The rest of these will go to family and friends.” She frosted a cookie for herself, then took a bite. Nodded. “Yep, this is a keeper.” She took another bite and licked the frosting that had gathered on her top lip. She looked up to find Adam watching her. “What did you want to talk about?”

“Uh…” He busied himself by doctoring his coffee with cream and sugar. “I know you got roped into this fund-raiser, so I won’t hold it against you if you want to bow out.”

Actually, after thinking about it, she realized that she was the perfect person to work on it. Like Rick said, she had a personal stake in seeing the fund-raiser do well, and she had a track record for successful events. And it would give her an outlet for her creativity and need to work. "I'm in. But if you want to quit..."

"I'm not quitting. In fact, I've come up with some ideas." He took another bite of a cookie leaving a touch of frosting on his top lip. "I was thinking a nice sit-down dinner at the VFW hall. Classy. Elegant. Desserts provided by you, of course. Perhaps a musical program."

"Nice try, but it's been done recently." She handed him a napkin. "I thought a bachelor or bachelorette auction might be fun. Different. I don't think we've had one of those in years."

Adam winced and wiped his mouth with the napkin. "I don't think so. That's tacky."

"Well, a dinner is boring."

He held up his hand. "Let's not start fighting before we even get this thing off the ground. How about we agree to consider all ideas before just dismissing them outright?"

"Agreed." She chose another cookie and took a bite of it without frosting it first.

It wasn't bad, but the frosting definitely added something extra to it. Kind of like her life without the bakery. "I also thought about throwing a talent show. There's nothing like a proud parent to buy up a bunch of tickets to make sure their little star gets seen by everyone and their brother."

He nodded. "What about a silent auction? We could go to businesses and community members for donations."

"Why not both?" She leaned back against the counter. "There's nothing that says we can only have one event."

"And we could combine them on the same evening. It might get people to one that might not go to the other." He used his long fingers to pick up the crumbs his cookies had left on his plate. "Doubles our chances for raising money. I like it."

"Anyone call you about joining the committee?" At his expression, she shrugged. "I guess memories are longer than you expected in Lake Mildred." She poured water in a kettle then put it on the burner to heat. "If it's any consolation, no one has called me, either."

"I probably could get my teller Eva to lend a hand."

"And I could talk to my sister. She's a talented singer, so she'd be an asset to work on the talent show." Megs turned back to face him. "If that's what we decide to do."

Adam grinned at her above the rim of his mug of coffee. "That's a great idea. Would she do it?"

"Without the Sweetheart, she's at loose ends, as well." Megs held up the coffee carafe. "More?"

He waved her off. "As good as it is, I think I need to decline. I'm on my way to the high school." He winced. "Giving a speech on bullying in front of the high school."

She nodded. "Bobby's challenge?" His eyebrows rose at this, and she said, "The whole town knows he called you out to do something. I didn't expect you would follow through."

"I have a lot to make up for, but thanks for the vote of confidence." He slid off the stool. "We should plan a time to meet to work on the fund-raiser."

"I thought that's what we were just doing."

"I need paper and a pen. Time to gather my thoughts. I guess I'm a type A that way. Needing to plan for a planning meeting."

She gave him a soft smile. "My schedule's pretty much wide-open, so anytime works for me."

"Why don't we say tomorrow night? At Rick's diner? Or would that be too busy a place for us to concentrate on this project?"

It was public, which made it perfect. "That would be fine." She took his mug, plate and spoon and added them to her growing pile to wash. "How about right after you close?"

"Five thirty."

She gave a nod. "Five thirty at Rick's." She walked him to the front door. "I'm glad you stopped by."

He turned and looked down at her. "Me, too." He waited as if wanting to say more, then gave a short shake of his head. "Thank you for the coffee and cookies. They really hit the spot before my big speech."

"My pleasure." And to her surprise, she found the words to be true. It had been a joy to serve him cookies that she had made with her own two hands, even if it had been in her own kitchen rather than the Sweetheart's. "I could give you some to take home."

He patted his flat stomach. "Thank you, but no. I appreciate the offer, but my trainer would not."

He didn't look as though he needed to work out, so tall and thin. He didn't have a very muscular build, but he was fit and lean. She followed the lines of his body up from his feet, past his legs and chest until she found him still looking at her. As if caught doing something wrong, she ducked her head. "I'll see you tomorrow."

He gave her a nod, and she shut the door before she could do something crazy. Like reaching out and touching the hard planes of his belly.

ADAM YANKED OFF his tie and suit jacket and folded them over the back of a chair in the high school principal's office. He unbuttoned the cuffs of his shirt and rolled the sleeves to his elbows. Was it warm in the office or was it just him? Mr. Lanigan, the principal, watched him as he settled into a seat across from him. "Please get comfortable now, Mr. Hawkins, because I can assure you that it won't be pleasant out there in the gym."

That was what he was nervous about. "I appreciate you letting me address them."

"I'll be honest. When I heard it was you, my first inclination was to refuse." Mr. Lanigan eyed him. "Bobby Snow is a friend of mine, and he warned me about all the stuff you did to him."

"I was a kid."

"And those are impressionable children in that room. I have an obligation to protect them." He flicked away invisible dust mites from the top of his desk. "But then you sent over what you intended to share, and I couldn't in good conscience refuse you." He held up the pages of Adam's email. "This is a story they need to hear."

Adam nodded. "I wish someone had shaken me up back then and warned me about the path I was on. It might have changed lives other than my own."

Mr. Lanigan rose. "Great. Then, let's not keep them in suspense any longer."

The principal escorted him down to the gymnasium, where the volume level had already hit a high. Adam paused just outside and took a deep breath before following Mr. Lanigan inside. He didn't look out into the packed bleachers at the students or the teachers. If he did, he'd lose his nerve. Instead, he concentrated on the floor as he walked to the middle of the basketball court, where a microphone stand waited for him. Mr. Lanigan quieted the crowd, then introduced Adam. He handed the microphone to him.

Adam grasped it in his hand and brought it up to his mouth. "As Mr. Lanigan said, I'm Adam Hawkins. Your principal has shared that the school has seen a rise in bullying. See, that's something I know about from experience. When I was a student here, I thought I was so cool since I was on the basketball team and track. I was tall and popular, which I thought meant I could do whatever I wanted." He stopped and shifted from one foot to the other. "And that included being a bully and hurting kids who weren't as cool as I thought I was."

A murmur broke out, and beads of sweat formed on Adam's forehead. He looked down at the ground. "I used names and words to hurt kids. I shoved them into lockers and the girls' bathroom. And I made their lives miserable because I could. And I dared anyone to stop me." A smile played around his lips. "One girl did stand up to me even though she was only half my height. She defended her friend who I was bullying, even though she knew she'd become a target herself. I wish there'd been more like her.

"I'm saying all this because I was angry and full of hate then. I was a bully because that was what happened to me at home. And I thought I could control what happened. I was wrong." He took a step forward. "Bullying, whether it's with your words or with your fists, is wrong. Doesn't matter if it's said in person or online, bullying destroys people and your school. It turns what could be the best years of your lives into misery."

He closed his eyes and hung his head. "I can't undo what I did back then no matter how hard I try." He opened his eyes and let his gaze settle on several kids in the crowd. "But I can encourage you to change now. If you're being bullied, speak up and tell someone. If you witness it happening to someone, stand up and defend them," he pleaded. "And if you're a bully, get help. You deserve a better life than that. Because all that hurt and anger will consume you."

He took a step back and offered the microphone to Mr. Lanigan. "Thank you, Mr. Hawkins. As part of what Adam's talking about, we have a pledge that you can pick up from the teachers on your way out. It states that by signing it, you promise to make Lake Mildred High a bully-free zone. That you will say something when you see bullying occurring in our hallways here as well as outside school and especially online. You're dismissed."

The kids stood up and started to file out of the gym. Adam spoke to Mr. Lanigan. "Do you think my speech will do any good?"

"Maybe."

"If I could stop just one kid…"

"Giving a speech to these kids is a nice idea. But if you really want to do something, you'd reach out and be a mentor to those who need help. Maybe even someone like you used to be."

"Be a mentor?" Adam wasn't convinced. "But I've got all the stuff happening at the bank and the fund-raiser—" He tried to think of an excuse. Mentoring a bully meant diving in even deeper into his issues. He offered lamely, "I'm busy."

"Right. Too busy to make a difference. I get it." And the principal walked out of the gym, leaving Adam staring after him.

Mentor a kid like him? What in the world could he possibly do to help a bully?

MEGS HAD PLENTY of time that Thursday afternoon before she had to meet with Adam. She'd baked several loaves of three-cheese bread, so she wrapped each in tissue paper and placed them in a canvas bag. She knew of several people who could use some bread.

The first place she drove to was Mr. Taber's house. He was elderly and lived on an extremely tight budget. She'd often dropped off extra baked goods when the bakery had been open. She noticed that his sidewalks were shoveled and salted, most likely the work of Will Stone's volunteer group. She knocked on the front door and waited. The door opened a crack, but didn't open until she held up a loaf of bread. "It's still warm."

Mr. Taber swung the door open and took the bread from her before letting her inside the house. "Been wondering what you've been up to without the Sweetheart."

He disappeared into the kitchen and returned with a knife and tub of margarine. He motioned to a threadbare recliner. "Have time to sit?"

"I have more deliveries to make." She took a sweeping glance of the living room. "Did you need me to pick up anything else while I'm out?"

He shook his head and stuffed the first hunk of bread into his mouth. "That Adam makes sure I'm taken care of. Though he'd be better off using his time helping those who really need it. I'm just fine."

"Adam?"

Mr. Taber swallowed. "Sure. He thinks I don't know it's him that keeps dropping bags of food off on my front porch, but I'd recognize his red pickup anywhere. He's not fooling nobody."

This wasn't the Adam that she knew.

But Mr. Taber was right. Adam's truck was pretty recognizable in a town of mostly black and white trucks. "I'd better go." She opened the front door and turned back. "Thank you, Mr. Taber."

He paused in his chewing. "What did I do?"

"Just being you."

The next stop was the motel by the freeway, where those who had been living in the apartments now stayed while arrangements could be made for new housing. She walked into the lobby and found the front-desk clerk watching a talk show on a small black-and-white television, his feet resting on the counter. As he saw her, he swung his legs down then stood. "Hi, Megs."

"Calvin, I brought some loaves of bread for the apartment residents." She placed the canvas bag on the counter, but took one loaf out for her last stop. "Could you see that everyone gets some?"

Calvin sniffed the air and nodded. He put one hand on the golden-brown crust of one loaf. "Your bread is good, but I've been missing your sticky buns. They're the best."

"Thank you. So you'll be sure that they get distributed?"

"You bet."

She took the last loaf to her car, then drove to a house not far from Main Street. She parked on the curb then glanced up. Hopefully, she'd catch Shelley, a harried single mother she knew from her high school days, at home and not away at one of her three jobs. Thursday afternoons usually meant she was home, and luck was on Megs's side.

Shelley answered the door, a baby sitting on one of her hips. "Hey, Megs. You caught me at a good time. I'm just making an early dinner for the kids."

Megs walked inside the tiny home to the kitchen, where three kids sat at the cracked Formica table. She held up the loaf of bread. "I happened to bake too many loaves again and thought you might like some."

Shelley took the loaf and held it up to her face and inhaled. "My favorite." She put the loaf on the table then returned to the stove where she stirred a pan of scrambled eggs. "Don't want these to burn."

"Do you want me to hold Hunter so you

can finish getting dinner ready?" When Shelley nodded, Megs took the baby from her and grimaced as he took a fistful of her hair.

"How have you been holding up without the Sweetheart?"

Megs attempted to remove her hair from the tight fist without making the baby fuss. "Oh, it's been a little quiet, but I'm working hard on getting it back in shape so we can reopen in April."

Shelley whistled and caught her eye. "That seems so far off, but it's really around the corner." She spooned eggs on paper plates, then clasped two in one hand and one in the other as she carried them to the table. She handed one to each child then found a serrated knife to cut the bread into thin slices. "Girls like us gotta keep busy."

"Certainly do. And everyone's been really supportive while I'm closed." She jiggled the baby, who attempted to grab her hair again. "Even Adam at the bank is helping me get a loan, and he's the last person I ever expected to lift a finger for me."

Shelley took the baby from Megs and put him in the highchair and slipped a bib on him before spooning some eggs on the tray. "That man has really changed since when we were in high school. He's been sending me money every month. Of course, he doesn't know that I know it's him."

Megs jaw dropped. "Are you sure it's him?"

"He showed up on my doorstep when he first got back to town. Said he wanted to apologize for all the things he said about me when it got out around school that I was pregnant with Trevor. Asked if there was anything he could do to make it up to me." She reached over and tousled the eleven-year-old's hair. "I could see it in his eyes that he was taking in the house and the bare cupboards and no husband and feeling bad. Sure enough, an envelope arrives a week later with a crisp one-hundred-dollar bill."

She smiled and put her arm across the back of Trevor's chair. "Now, I've got my pride, but that money helped feed my kids, so I wasn't going to throw it back in his face. Then two weeks later, another envelope and another hundred-dollar bill. Been arriving like that ever since. And on Christmas Eve, a garbage bag full of toys and clothes for the kids appears on my doorstep." She looked over at Megs. "He is a changed man. And changed for the better."

Megs glanced at the kitchen clock. "I hate to cut my visit short, but I have an appointment that I need to get to." She gave Shelley a quick hug. "If you need anything, just call."

She mulled over everything Shelley had told her about Adam as she drove to Rick's diner. People could change, and maybe he had. When she entered the diner, she spotted Adam sitting at a booth near the back. She took a deep breath and told herself she could do this. As she went over to join him, she gave a small wave to Rick, who rested against the counter. He nodded at her then came around with a glass of ice water. "I've got city chicken with mashed potatoes."

Was she that predictable? She gave a nod as she removed her coat and flung it toward the back of the booth along with her hat and scarf. "And a salad with…" She paused as she took a seat, then shrugged. "Raspberry vinaigrette."

Rick raised an eyebrow then looked over

at Adam. He gave a nod. “The same, but I’ll take ranch dressing on my salad.”

Megs held up her finger. “I changed my mind. Ranch on mine, too.”

Rick gave her a smile. “You were starting to worry me. I thought I’d forgotten my customer’s preferences.”

“I thought about changing it up, but…” She unwrapped a straw and glanced over at Adam who was watching her. “Grammy and I ate here quite a bit. And we always ordered the same thing.” She raised a brow, asking, “I like my routines, okay?”

“I didn’t say there was anything wrong with that.” He reached out and touched her hand. “I’m not criticizing you.”

She took her hand away from his. “Forgive me if that’s not what I’m used to from you.” She gave Rick a smile as he brought their salads and a bread basket. She waited until he had left before turning back to Adam. “Just so you know, I’m trying hard to forgive you, but I haven’t forgotten, and I’m not likely to.”

He cleared his throat and sat up stiffer on his side of the booth. “I’m not asking you to. I know I can’t make up for our past, but

I'm trying to show you that I've changed. I'm not the same boy you remember. I've grown up."

And he had, physically at least. It was whether he had changed from the bully she had known that she couldn't be sure of. After hearing Shelley's story, she wondered if she might be wrong about him. She unrolled her napkin and placed it on her lap before picking at her salad. "This is why I insisted on not talking about our past." She glanced up at him, then dropped her gaze back to her plate. "It gets complicated."

"Tell me about it."

They remained silent as they ate their salads. She knew she was being a spoiled brat. Was it so hard to let go of the past? She certainly wasn't the girl who had risked everything to stand up to a bully. For another, she'd learned that people lied to get what they wanted. That they would hurt you to make them look better in front of their friends. She was the only person she could depend on.

All lessons learned because of the man sharing a meal with her.

She pushed her salad plate to the side and

fiddled with the straw in her drink. "Let's just discuss the fund-raiser ideas and what we need to do and when."

"Keep it professional."

She nodded. "I talked to my sister, Kelly, who agreed to help us with the talent show if we go that route. She even volunteered to emcee it with her boyfriend, Sam."

Adam made notes on the legal pad beside him. "Thank goodness because I wasn't sure about doing that myself. Giving that speech at the town hall meeting was nerve-racking enough. I can't imagine having to host an event."

"I talked to Heather, the library director, and she said we can use the meeting room for the event if we want. But we probably need a bigger auditorium or a theater or something." She took a sip of her water. "This might be a crazy idea, but I wondered if we could get the new owner of the theater to donate it for one night. He's talking about renovating it later this spring, but we might be able to use it since it's just sitting empty."

Adam frowned. "Who owns the theater now?"

"Some guy from out of town. Haven't

met him, but people say he seems nice." She waited as Rick set their plates of city chicken in front of them. Then she scooped a healthy portion of mashed potatoes onto her fork. "It would give us more seats, which means more ticket sales, which means more money for the bottom line."

Adam wrote this down and put several question marks after it. "What about the auditorium at the high school? It seemed like a good size."

"True, but they charge for the use of it." She paused in eating and cocked her head to the side. "Same with the VFW hall. Worse comes to worse, we go with the library. But I'd like to see a bigger venue."

"And you think we can fill all those seats?"

She swallowed the mouthful of potato heaven. "Like I said, parents will buy huge sections of tickets to show their talented kid off."

"Well, I talked to Eva about donations we could get for the silent auction." He flipped through the legal pad and found the page he wanted. "She volunteered her group of seniors to help out with anything we need. Whether it's getting donations or finding talent, she said they'll lend a hand."

Megs nodded. "Sounds as though we've decided on our two events, then." She dragged her fork through the gravy. "I could contact the school choir directors to let them know about the show. And Heather said we can post signs at the library to advertise."

Adam made more notes. "Looks as if this is really coming together."

"The community is willing to help each other out, so I'm expecting a good turnout." She paused as she cut up her city chicken. "My concern is getting enough donations for the silent auction and acts for the talent show. The rest of it will take care of itself."

"We have ideas of where to start, though. We'll just have to have faith that people will step up like you said." He put his pen down and tucked into his dinner.

She supposed that was the best thing to do before it got cold, so she did the same. But she kept an eye out in case Adam had any more ideas about bringing up their past again.

THAT WOMAN WAS too wary of him. Granted, he'd given her enough reasons himself for her to be cautious around him. But just once, he wished that she'd give him the benefit of the doubt and trust him, if even just a little bit. What did he have to do to redeem himself to her? Short of asking her point-blank, he was out of ideas.

He finished his meal and pushed his plate away. Some of the best city chicken he'd ever had. He picked up the legal pad and read over his notes. "I bet if we work together, we can do what we need to do pretty quickly. Maybe hold the event on a weekend in March."

Megs frowned, and he wanted to reach over and smooth away those lines from her forehead. She was too young to get wrinkles. "We'll get more done if we split things up and work independently. I'll take on the talent show with my sister. You can work on donations from the community."

"Yes, ma'am."

He flipped to a fresh page and made a list of places he could contact. Megs watched him, then pointed to a name. "He moved to

Florida last year. Scratch him off your list." Another name. "He died, and she moved in with her kids in Seattle two years ago."

"That's why I need your help on this, obviously." He slid the legal pad over to her. "Where do I go from here?"

Megs picked up the pen and added a few businesses, including Shane's aquarium shop. When he pointed to the name, she shrugged. "He has inventory just sitting there. He might be willing."

"Then, you'll have to be the one to ask him. If I do, it's an automatic no."

She sighed. "I'll check with him later this week."

"Thanks."

He watched her write a few more names, then got out her cell phone and looked up their numbers. Her blond bangs fell over her forehead, and his fingers twitched, tempted to reach out and brush the hair aside. But that would definitely break one of her rules. She glanced up at him then pushed the pad of paper back across the table. "That should get you started."

She gave him a smile, and his heart felt

as if it would overload with the wattage that came from it. He grinned back at her, then took the pen from her fingers. "I'm glad you're helping me on this."

"It's for the community."

Their waitress, Shirley, came and cleared the table, then returned with her order pad. "Did you save room for dessert?"

Megs patted her flat belly. "Oh, I don't think I could."

Shirley leaned against the table. "Ernesto made his coconut-cream pie today, and I just put on a fresh pot of coffee."

Adam held up two fingers. "We'll each take both."

Shirley left before Megs could protest. He shrugged at her. "I'm having a nice time with you. Maybe I don't want it to end." He flipped to another blank page. "Besides, we've got the donations list covered, but the talent show is going to require as much, if not more, work."

"I told you. Kelly and I have got that covered."

"Then, what else do you want to discuss over pie?"

Shirley brought over their dessert and

clean forks, as well as the pot of coffee. Adam waited while she poured before taking a deep breath and plunging ahead. "Have you heard anything about Kenny's parents? I can't seem to find a number for them."

Megs's eyes widened. "Why don't you let it go? I said I didn't want to talk about him."

"I'm not talking about him. I'm asking if you know where his parents are."

"Why would you need to know that?"

Because he had amends to make, apologies to offer. "I looked them up in the phone book, but they're not listed."

"Because they got divorced, and Mr. Pierce moved away." Megs fiddled with her fork, plunking it in the whipped cream. "Mrs. Pierce is still in town, but she got remarried last I heard." She looked up at him, her eyes full of pain. "She comes into the bakery sometimes, but I don't wait on her."

"Why not?"

"I can't look her in the eyes after what happened." She kept her gaze on the pie, refusing to meet his own eyes. "So I let someone else take care of her."

He reached across the table and touched

her free hand. "You did nothing to be ashamed of."

She finally lifted her head to stare at him. "What do you know about it?"

"I was there, too."

She removed her hand from his, then stood, grabbing her coat from the booth and stuffing her arms inside. "I can't talk about Kenny. Especially with you of all people. Maybe us working together is a bad idea."

He rose to his feet and stepped in the path of her exit. "I need to talk about him, about our history. I can't get past it otherwise. And I really want us to be able to move beyond that day."

Tears spilled from her hazel eyes and down her pale cheeks. She shook her head and crossed her arms over her chest. "I'm sorry. I can't."

She brushed past him and ran out of the diner into the night. Adam slumped back into the booth and pushed his plate of pie away, no longer hungry.

He pictured Kenny in his mind as he'd been that November day. He'd been wearing a flannel shirt over a T-shirt and black jeans. Thick glasses. Dark, unkempt hair that probably needed washing. Normal for the kid, but Adam had lit on him, mocking his clothes and messy appearance. Calling him names. Then Megs had pushed her way between them, yelled at Adam for picking on someone weaker than himself.

It had been the last time he'd seen Kenny before his funeral. The kid had killed himself later that day after school.

And Adam had been trying to pay penance for it ever since.

MEGS RESTED HER head against the steering wheel of her car, letting the tears come in chest-shaking sobs. Why had he had to bring Kenny up? Couldn't he have just left the past alone? Why drag it all up again?

Kenny had been her friend since her dad had died and mom had taken off when she was twelve. He'd handed her tissues when she'd cried and held her hand when she couldn't. But he'd never shared his own troubles with her. If she hadn't overheard the awful things Adam had been saying to him, she wouldn't have known he'd been bullied.

Maybe if she hadn't stood up to Adam, her friend might still be alive. But she had, and instead of thanking her for getting his bully to back off, Kenny had accused her of making things worse. He'd said she'd put a bigger target on his chest, that Adam would never stop until Kenny was dead.

And then he was gone.

Her life had never been the same since that day. She'd lived her life according to new rules so that no one else close to her would get hurt. That she'd be able to redeem her sins with Kenny by being the perfect granddaughter, sister, student and employee. She'd succeeded at it, too, but Adam coming back to town only reminded her of how much further she had to go to make up for Kenny's death.

A rap on her window brought her head up, and she paused to wipe the tears from her eyes before she turned to find Adam peering in on her. She rolled the window down. "What do you want now?"

He leaned farther down so that his eyes were on the same level as hers. "Are you okay?"

She bit her lip, but didn't answer. Only

gave a nod and started her car. "I have to go home."

"You shouldn't drive this upset. Not on these icy roads."

"I'll be fine." She started to roll her window back up, but he placed his hand on the top edge so that she couldn't without smashing his fingers. "I want to go home."

"I'll drive you."

She shook her head. "I also want to be alone." She needed to be by herself so she could pack that awful day in her memory and leave it there, rather than bringing it out to examine. "Let go of my window."

Adam sighed and removed his hand but went to stand in front of her car. "Megan, stop being so stubborn. I'll drive you home and not say a word the entire trip, if that's what you want."

The roads looked bad, and out in the country where she lived they'd be worse. She touched the key resting in the ignition, weighing her options. Adam wasn't going to let go of this, much like he did with everything else. He'd pester her until she was in the passenger seat of his truck.

She shut off the car and grabbed the

handle of her purse. She got out of the car and hit the key fob twice to lock the doors. "Fine. I'll have my sister drive me out in the morning to pick up my car."

Adam nodded, then led her to where his truck waited down the street in the parking lot of the bank. He opened the door for her and helped boost her inside. She reached over her right shoulder and pulled the seat belt strap across her body and clicked it into place. Then she scooted as close to the window as she could get, anything to be farther from Adam's presence. He could drive her home, but this wouldn't be a pleasant car ride.

Adam hopped up into the driver's seat, then turned the key in the ignition to make the truck growl to life. He cast a glance at her before putting the truck in gear, and she in turn gazed out her window.

She couldn't look at him. Couldn't see the reminder of her biggest regret.

True to his word, no words were spoken between them on the ride back to Grammy's house. The only sound was the radio tuned to a classic-rock station. A song from their high school years played. She just couldn't escape her past, no matter what she did, could she?

After crawling along the icy roads for fifteen minutes, Adam pulled into the driveway of the farmhouse. He had barely put it in Park before she'd ripped off the seat belt and opened the passenger door, hopping down into the snow and running for the side door into the kitchen. She slammed the door behind her then leaned back, closing her eyes and willing her heart to slow down.

"Everything okay?"

Megs opened her eyes and saw Kelly and Sam sitting at the kitchen island going over some paperwork. She gave a short nod. "The roads were bad, so I left my car in town and got a ride home. Can you take me to pick up my vehicle in the morning?"

"Absolutely." Kelly slid off the stool and approached her. She hugged her for a long moment. "You're shaking. What's wrong?"

"Nothing." She maneuvered out of her sister's arms and left the kitchen, unzipping her coat on the way into the foyer. She hung the coat on a peg next to the others, then paused before re-entering the kitchen, pasting a noncommittal smile on her face. "The plans for the fund-raiser are really coming along. But I'll need help with recruiting acts for the talent show."

Kelly said, "I promised you I'd do whatever I could." She gestured to Sam. "And I promised your help, too."

"Whatever you need, Megs." He gathered the papers and put them in a manila folder. "But your sister's right. You're pale and shaking. Do I need to have a stern talk with our neighborhood banker?"

As if that would make things better. "It's nothing I can't handle."

"He didn't put any moves on you?"

She almost laughed at the protective look on Sam's face. "No. It's nothing like that. Just some history between us."

Sam's eyebrows rose almost to his hairline. "That's news to me. I didn't realize there was ever anything romantic between you two."

"Who said anything about romantic? I would never date anyone like him. Ever." She slammed her purse on the kitchen island.

Kelly glanced at Sam then Megs. "You know what they say, right? Never say never."

"Well, I mean it. And I don't want to talk about Adam." She glanced between them. "I'm tired and going to bed. Good night."

She walked up to her bedroom, then collapsed on the bed, staring up at the ceiling. Her phone chimed, indicating she'd received a text. Sorry for this evening. I didn't mean to make you cry.

She didn't have to look at the number to know whom it was from. She pressed the delete button, then turned on her side, pulling the quilted comforter around her. Sleep, that was what she needed. Sleep and to forget. Tomorrow was a new day, and she'd be able to face it with courage if she could forget the past.

ADAM COULDN'T FORGET the look on Megan's face the night before when he'd brought up Kenny's name. He should have kept his thoughts to himself, paid his penance quietly rather than trying to rope her into it, as well. He parked along Lincoln in front of Shane's aquarium shop. Inside, it was still dark, so he'd probably missed his opportunity to try to talk the man into working with him on a loan.

So many victims for him to make amends with.

He glanced next door at the Sweetheart bakery and saw activity inside. He walked over and opened the front door, poking his head inside. Scaffolding filled the front room, and he leaned back to glance up to where a man worked on reinforcing the roof beams. “Megs around?”

The man finished using the nail gun to keep the supports in place, then leaned over the side. “She’s not on-site today. I told her to stay out of my way so I can get this done before the rest of the roofing crew gets down to this end.”

A not so subtle hint that Adam himself was interfering with the work. “She’s not answering my phone calls or texts.”

“Maybe you should take the hint.” Sam turned back to look up at the roof. “She’s got enough going on without having to deal with you, too.”

“We’re working on the fund-raiser together, so she can’t ignore me.”

“I know what she’s doing with you.” Sam

cleared his throat. "Listen, Adam, I'm relatively new to town so I'm not aware of all your history. But Megs is like my sister, and I see how upset she gets around you. Maybe you should give her some space."

"I'm working on her loan as well as organizing the fund-raiser with her. Space is the last thing we can afford right now." He ran a hand through his hair. "Did she tell you what happened?"

Sam frowned. "I've heard her side." He looked him over. "Do you want to tell me yours?"

"Not really." The only person he wanted to talk to about it wouldn't let him even bring up the topic. And he needed to find out what she remembered about that day.

"Why are you working so hard for this community fund anyway? I mean, the bank already offered the loans and everything. Why work on this?"

Adam was unsure of how much to share. "I guess because I spent most of my youth trying to destroy this place. Now I want to help rather than hurt."

Sam gave a nod at that. "I'll be sure to tell her you're looking for her."

"Thank you. She can't avoid me forever."

"Unfortunately, that's likely part of her plan." Sam put his goggles back over his eyes. "Don't let the door hit you on the way out."

Dismissed, Adam left and went back to his car and got inside. He took out his cell phone and pulled up Megan's name. Where are you? I need to see you, please.

He put his truck in gear, then drove back to the bank, giving her time to respond. He parked at the back of the bank's parking lot, then walked briskly inside. He gave a nod to Eva, then retreated to his office. He put his cell phone on his desk, feeling like a teenage boy waiting for his crush to notice him. He shook his head.

The phone buzzed, and his heart leaped in his chest. Okay. Where?

The fact that she wanted to meet with him shouldn't have made him feel as good as it did. Neutral ground. The theater at 6?

There was no immediate response. He sighed and ran a hand through his hair. They needed to talk to the owner anyway about using the place for the talent show.

Maybe kill two birds at once. Be more efficient.

K.

Not much of a response, but he'd take it. He turned on his computer and searched for the theater owner's phone number. Hopefully they'd be able to tour the place, too.

MEGS HUDDLED IN her car and stared up at the entrance of the theater. Why had she agreed to meet with Adam again? She could have told him everything that he needed to know over the phone. But after the sixth phone call, she'd caved. He claimed that he was sorry for bringing up Kenny again.

But the thing was, they needed to talk about him. Had to get past that one day that seemed to hold her back from living her life. The guilt of that day and the aftermath.

She took a deep breath and glanced at the dashboard. 5:56. There was only one car in the parking lot, but no sign of Adam's truck. She turned the heater down a notch and turned the volume up on the radio. She loved this song. She bobbed her head and sang along for a moment, closing her eyes and letting herself enjoy the tune.

The knock on her window stopped her private concert. She peered out and saw Adam smiling down at her. She cut the engine, grabbed her purse and hopped out of the car. "I got here early."

"Good song?"

The heat rose on her cheeks and she pushed past him to get to the entrance of the theater. He hurried and got there first, opening the door wide for her. She nodded at him before entering. Ignored the feeling in her belly caused by the woodsy scent emanating from his skin as she brushed past him. She stopped in the foyer to let her eyes adjust to the lower lighting, then spotted the new theater owner polishing the brass staircase railing. He wore a flannel shirt and jeans and looked more like a cowboy than a theater person. He paused in his work and waved with his rag at them. "You made it."

Megs walked to the foot of the sweeping red carpeted staircase that led to the balcony of the theater. She put her foot on the first step and waited as the owner descended. “Mr. Scott?”

After wiping his hands on the rag, he shook her outstretched hand. “It’s Bryan, please. I hear Mr. Scott and turn to see if my father is standing there.”

Megs gave him a smile. “Bryan, then.” She looked around the foyer and whistled. “It’s amazing in here.”

He shook Adam’s hand. “You wouldn’t believe the condition this old lady was in when I found her. But luckily I have more money and time on my hands than I know what to do with, so I’m giving her a colossal makeover. Would you two like the deluxe tour?”

They nodded and followed him as he took them first to the balcony that overlooked the stage, then each of the eight private boxes. They saw the green room backstage, then took a walk out on the stage itself that extended out into the empty audience. Bryan grimaced. “The seats still need to be reupholstered, but she’s come a long way.”

“Will the theater be ready for a talent show by next month?” Megs glanced out at the seats, some missing backs and arms. "We're holding a fund-raiser for the people affected by the roof collapse downtown, and we're looking for a big enough venue."

Bryan gave a big sigh. "How soon?"

Adam held his hand up. "The dates are tentative, but we could find a compromise if you need more time. That is, if you're willing to donate the use of the theater."

"I'd be happy to help the community, but a month?" He whistled. "I'm the only one working on fixing up this place right now."

"I could give you a hand if it will help our case." Adam looked around and gave a shrug. "I worked my way through college by doing odd construction jobs."

"Well, fixing this place up is definitely odd in the jobs." He nodded his head toward the back of the stage. "You wouldn't believe the things I found stored in closets and under the stage. And every time I complete one job, three more pop up."

"I'll volunteer my time to help you."

"All right, then." Bryan held out a hand, and they shook on it. "You help me get this place ready in a month, and it's yours for your show."

"Thank you, Mr.…Bryan." Megs moved to the edge of the stage and tried to picture the talent this theater could hold. Her eyelids fluttered closed, she could almost hear their sweet voices singing.

A throat cleared behind her, and she turned to find Bryan gone and Adam watching her. "This place is perfect," she said.

He nodded and joined her at the edge. "That's why I agreed to help him." When she frowned at him, he shrugged. "It's not as if I have a social life right now. What else was I going to do?"

"Why are you working so hard to be the nice guy in town?"

"Isn't it obvious?" He looked out into the audience. "I'm paying for my past sins."

She stared up at him, but he wouldn't gaze in her direction. "You want to talk about Kenny."

At the name, he turned to her. "He gets to me, too, you know. The names I called him, the words I said. They taunt me when I lie down at night." His eyes glistened, and she stepped away. "I've tried so hard to shed the bad boy and become the good man that I should have been all along."

"It's not your fault he died."

"Maybe if I hadn't pushed him that far, he'd still be here."

"You're not the guilty one. I am." She wiped the tears from her face, then walked offstage and down into the audience.

ADAM STARED AFTER Megs, trying to make sense of this. She was the responsible one? Why was she letting him off the hook? He followed her and found her sitting in a seat in the last row of the auditorium. She looked up at him as he approached, tears staining her cheeks. He took a seat a few down from her, then turned to look at her. "What did you do to Kenny but stand up for him?"

"That's why he killed himself. I should have kept quiet." She covered her face and bent over at the waist, heart-rending sobs coming from deep within her.

Adam rose and claimed the seat next to her. He put his arm around her shoulders, and she turned into his embrace. Her tears dampened the lapels of his wool coat as she clung to him and wept. He rested his chin on top of her blond head. "You were the best friend he had. He couldn't have asked for better."

"But you still bullied him after I stood up to you."

"Then, that's on me, not you." He would take those words back if he could, but once spoken they couldn't be recalled. "I'm the guilty one here. And I've been working to redeem myself ever since. Not that I've ever come close."

"How do you get rid of the guilt? I haven't found a way. A decade later, and it's still as if it was yesterday."

"I don't think you ever really get rid of it." He tightened his arms around her. The floral scent of her shampoo teased his nose as he held her close and breathed her in. "But maybe we can find ways to ease its sting."

Her sobs had stopped, her eyes rimmed in red and full of pain. "How? Because I've lived with it every day since he died."

Adam squeezed tighter. "So have I. But I promised myself that I would become a decent person, someone others could respect. I've worked hard and I've tried to atone for my sins by reaching out to make amends.

Even if it's only an apology." He brushed her bangs away from her forehead. "That's why I want to reach out to Kenny's parents. To apologize and see if there is anything I can do for them."

She gave a nod then sat back and wiped her eyes. "That makes sense." She accepted the handkerchief he held out to her and dried her tears. "Maybe we could go together."

"You don't have anything to atone for, Megan. I'm the one who pushed him to do it."

She shook her head and twisted the handkerchief. "I know what Kenny said to me. He blamed me for you bullying him even more."

"That doesn't make you responsible."

"It does in my book." She looked at the handkerchief in her hands. "I'll wash this and get it back to you."

"That's okay. I can wash it."

She kept her grip on it. "No, I want to do that for you. I appreciate that you let me use it."

"Do you think you're okay now?"

She nodded, then stood. "Maybe I was

wrong. Maybe I needed to talk about him, too. The burden isn't gone, but it feels lighter."

"Mine, too." He gave her a smile, and the warm feeling spread from his belly to his fingertips when she returned it in kind.

CHAPTER SIX

AFTER THEIR DISCUSSION about Kenny, Megs found it much easier to look at Adam and not experience the tugging guilt from before. She even looked forward to meeting with him today to sign the final paperwork for her loan application. She'd baked a coffee-cake ring for him and his staff since she had supplies that would spoil if she didn't use them. And since her business remained closed, she had been spending her mornings baking everything from pastries to bread. Some she froze to use later for the fund-raiser. Most she gave away.

As she entered the lobby, she gave Mrs. Stone a wave before approaching her teller window. She placed the box with the pastry on the counter. "I brought you a coffee-cake ring for the staff."

Eva lifted the lid and grinned. "It smells great, and probably tastes even better."

"I'm trying to stay busy." She glanced behind her at the closed door of Adam's office. "I'm early for my appointment. Does he have a customer or is he free?"

Eva placed the pastry box on the back counter. "A customer, and not one of his favorites." She glanced around the empty bank lobby. "Can I get you some coffee or water while you're waiting? Maybe a slice of this great cake?"

Megs held up her hand. "No, I'm good. I'll just take a seat and wait for him."

"I'll let him know you're here." Eva typed on her computer, then disappeared with the pastry box down a hall where Megs assumed the break room was located.

Megs took a seat on one of the chairs in the waiting area and placed her purse in her lap. She hoped Adam's appointment was going well so that he'd be in a good mood. She needed to discuss not only the loan paperwork but their efforts on the fund-raiser. She'd had some success reaching out to the local music teachers as well as some of the church choirs in the community. She already had seven people sign up for the talent show.

Adam's office door opened, and an older man appeared in the doorway. "I can pull my money from this bank anytime I want, sonny. So maybe you'd better rethink your interest rates."

The man stuffed a hat on his head, then stormed out of the branch. Megs peered inside the office and saw Adam sitting at the desk, his head in his hands. He took a few deep breaths, then stood. His smile at her looked strained, yet genuine. "Megan, can I have two minutes before we meet?"

"Take all the time you need."

"Thanks." He stood and walked out of his office and down the hall. In a moment, he returned with a thermos and a slice of her coffee cake on a paper plate. "You made this?"

She stood and smiled. "I thought you and your staff might appreciate something sweet today."

"Today. Tomorrow. Anytime." He broke off a piece and popped it into his mouth. As he chewed, his eyes drifted closed. "This is amazing."

"Thanks."

He opened his eyes and motioned her

into his office. After a few sips from his thermos, he then placed it and his plate of half-eaten pastry on the desk before sitting behind it. "Man, I really needed that. Thank you."

"You're welcome." She sat and gave him a smile, pleased that he enjoyed her baking so much. "It really is my pleasure."

"Well, it's my delight to eat it." He took another bite, then pulled out a file and started to organize papers into piles on his desk. He swallowed. "As we talked about, the only remaining condition that the loan consultant placed on your application is to have a cosigner."

How could she forget the crazy restrictions they had placed on her? In response, she pulled out an envelope from her purse and handed it to him. "As promised, these are the financials for my cosigner, Sam. He said if you need anything else to let him know, and he can drop it off. He should be here any minute to sign the paperwork."

Adam pulled out several sheets of paper from the envelope and perused them. "These look good and should satisfy the loan consultant."

She smiled. At least one thing was going right in this process. Though she'd hated to ask Sam for his assistance, she hadn't had much of a choice. But as he'd said, he was like family to her and was more than willing to lend a helping hand. "Once we sign these preliminary papers, how long until I get the funds for my reconstruction?"

Adam placed the pages face up on his desk. "It's not going to be overnight, Megan. As much as I wish I could, it will still be about two weeks or so for this to come out of underwriting and we issue you a check."

Oh. She gave a nod though she had really been hoping that she would receive a fat check sooner than that. "But you think we'll be able to close the loan in two weeks?"

"I'm hoping so."

Once Sam arrived, Adam led them through the forms and got their signatures a million times it seemed. Once they had signed the last document, he put them in a certain order, then stood. "I'll get these scanned and emailed right now. Can you wait five minutes for me, Megan? There's something else I was hoping we could discuss."

Sam stood. "I've got to get back to the bakery." He shook hands with Adam, then turned to Megs. "See you in a bit."

ADAM RETURNED TO his office from the scanner with the papers in his hand and found Sam already gone and Megan on her phone, probably with her sister.

"Two weeks, he said." She looked up at him and held up a finger. "True, but we can start on some things while we're waiting." She ended the conversation with a promise to call later, then focused on him. While she'd been on the phone, he'd been watching her, admiring the way the light came in and hit the golden highlights of her hair. He blinked twice. Oh, right. He pulled out the legal pad with his notes for the fundraiser from his desk drawer and pushed it across the desk to her. "I'm striking out on the donations from community members."

Megan studied his notes, frowning. "Mr. Thomas turned you down? And Mrs. Swift, too?" She shook her head and looked up at him. "This can't be right. They're huge supporters in the community. They're always looking for ways to give back."

"Well, they both turned me down flat." More than turning him down, they'd doubted his reformed reputation. "It could be the way I'm asking or..."

"Or they could be holding your past against you." Megan pulled his phone across the desk toward her and lifted the receiver. She dialed the first number then waited. After greeting the person on the other line, she explained her work with the fund-raising committee and asked for a donation of a free golf game. She smiled and thanked them before hanging up.

How did she make it look so easy? He'd been calling and even stopping by several businesses, but hadn't gotten much except for a polite no thank you. "Mr. Thomas?"

Megan nodded and marked the donation on the second sheet with the few items listed. "He said he didn't realize I was working with you. He's more than happy to help out."

Adam groaned and ran a hand through his hair.

"I can see how this might be a problem."

She glanced through the rest of the list. "Do you have plans tonight?"

"I was hoping to help Bryan at the theater for a few hours. I promised I'd help him fix the seats." And he didn't break his promises anymore.

"Right, I forgot." She glanced at her watch. "Maybe I could meet you here at closing, and we could make some stops before going to the theater?"

"You're planning on soliciting these businesses for me?"

"With you, not for you." She made a few notes on the list, then looked up at him, her eyes filled with determination and something else. Something that reminded him of hope. "Maybe if they see us together, they won't turn us down so quick."

"You are hard to say no to."

She smiled at that and stood, retrieving her purse and coat. "And if I come with some pastries, they'll have an even harder time of refusing our request." She put on her hat. "I've got some baking to do, but I'll meet you back here at five."

"Make it five thirty." He stood and walked her to the door. He put a hand on her shoulder before she could leave. "Thank you for helping me with this."

"I'm doing this for the community."

"Right." But he was disappointed that she hadn't done it for his sake.

MEGS ARRIVED AT the bank just before five thirty and waited in her car while the employees left the branch. Adam locked the doors, then waved as everyone walked to their cars. He surveyed the parking lot and spotted her car next to his truck. She rolled the window down as he approached her car. "Why don't we go in my truck? They're predicting another few inches tonight, and I've got snow tires."

So did she, but her car was lightweight while his truck was solid and wouldn't have them skidding on the roads. She gave a nod and popped the button for her trunk. "We'll have to move the pastry boxes to your truck, then."

He lifted the trunk lid and whistled. "How many businesses did you think we'd visit tonight?"

Okay, so she'd gone a little crazy with the cookies, cakes and pies, not to mention tarts and bread. She shrugged. “Enough of them to get a good list of donations. You can take home a few boxes of pastries if we have any left over.”

“I’ll hold you to that offer.” He helped her to load the boxes into the back of his truck. He looked at the boxes, then at her. “Do you think they’ll be okay here?”

“As long as you don’t swerve all over the road.” She put in the last box, then waited for him to slam shut the tailgate. She moved to the passenger side and waited as he came around to help boost her into the seat. She really disliked being this short, but it was the way she’d been born.

Adam ran around the truck and got in on the other side. He started the truck, and it growled to life. She put on her seat belt and pulled out the list she’d made of places to visit. “I figured we’d hit businesses on Main Street first. They were near enough to the damaged ones to feel the effect that our being closed has had. They might be more willing to donate to our cause.”

He nodded and put the truck in gear. They stayed silent while he drove toward the center of town and parked near city hall. Megs checked her watch. She figured they had about ninety minutes before places closed for the night. Not including the department store Roxy's, which would be open until nine. She grabbed the notebook and her purse before hopping down from the truck. Adam had already retrieved three pastry boxes tied with string.

"Okay, where to first?"

She knew they needed an easy mark for the first one, so she chose Threads, Martha's dress shop. She had known Martha since she'd been a teenager and had admired the older woman for how she'd raised her son, Jeff, who had Down's syndrome. She had a soft heart as well as a weakness for the Sweetheart's chocolate éclairs. Megs walked with purpose to the dress shop and pulled the door opened. A bell above the door announced their arrival. Martha popped her head out of one of the dressing rooms near the back. "Be right there."

Adam shifted his weight and glanced around the store. "This had to be our first stop?"

"Martha has a good heart as well as a generous one."

"Okay, but this is definitely out of my comfort zone." He picked up a scarf and let the silky material fall back onto the counter near the register. "Now, put me in a sporting goods or an outdoor living store, and you've got my number."

Martha walked out from the dressing room and hung some items of clothing on the rack next to the register. "Why, Megs, I wasn't expecting you today. Are you looking for something special?" She gave Megs a bright smile, then turned a speculative look at Adam.

Megs shook her head. "Actually, Adam and I are on the Lincoln Street fund-raising committee together and we're hoping you'd have something to donate for our silent auction next month."

"How much do you need?" Martha glanced around the store and walked across the aisle to pull a beautiful mohair sweater in a shade of blue that reminded Megs of sapphires. "I just got some of these sweaters in and could put together an outfit. Or perhaps a gift certificate or two."

"We would appreciate whatever you can donate. The fund-raiser is important to more than just the business owners on Lincoln."

Martha nodded. "I'll put some things together and have them to you by the end of the month."

"Thank you, Martha." Megs turned and took the top box from Adam's hands. "As a token of our gratitude, I brought pastries."

"Éclairs?"

"And I can bring more when I pick up your donations."

Martha took the pastry box and nodded. "Jeff will be so excited to see me bring these home. He's been missing the Sweetheart something awful."

"I've missed seeing him, too. Give him my love?"

Once outside, Adam whistled. "Like I said, you made that look easy."

"I've served on a couple of committees with Grammy in this town." She gave a shrug as if it was no big deal. "So I've had experience pounding the pavement for donations."

"I'm glad you're on my side." He shifted the boxes to his other arm. "Where to now?"

Megs paused. "You said Mrs. Swift turned

you down, but I thought we'd give her another chance to help out."

Adam slipped his free hand in hers and squeezed. "If you're going with me, I don't see how we can lose."

She hoped he was right.

MRS. SWIFT'S BOOKSTORE seemed a re-creation from the pages of one of Charles Dickens's novels. Floor-to-ceiling bookshelves crammed with volumes. A comfy nook with overstuffed chairs. A white longhair cat, who flicked its tail at them from its perch behind the register. Adam took a deep breath and smelled paper and ink. He almost broke out in hives.

Mrs. Swift looked up from the novel she was reading and adjusted her eyeglasses. "Mr. Hawkins." Her tone was cool, almost chilly. But when Megan walked in behind him, she greeted her more warmly. "Ms. Sweet, I haven't seen you in weeks."

Megan gave an embarrassed giggle. "You'd think with the bakery closed that I'd have more time on my hands to read."

"That new cookbook you wanted should

arrive next month once it's released. I'll be sure to give you a call."

Megan replied, "I'd appreciate that." She glanced at Adam then back at Mrs. Swift. "I believe you spoke with my friend Adam a few days ago about the fund-raiser we're holding for the Lincoln Street businesses."

"Yes, I think I remember that."

"Good, then I was hoping we could put you down for a bigger donation than you had already pledged."

Adam glanced at her. The woman had turned him down flat, not promised anything. What kind of game was Megan playing? But he didn't say a word, letting her handle the old bat.

"Oh." Mrs. Swift sniffed and glanced around the bookstore. "What was it I had promised?"

"We were hoping for more than a boxed set of books. Perhaps a gift certificate or two, as well?" Megan gave the old woman a bright smile. "I know how you look forward to giving back to the community. Especially when you can use your influence to educate and inform your neighbors."

The old woman gave a deep sigh. "Well, yes, given that it's for such a good cause."

"Absolutely. I knew I could count on you. Adam being back in town has been such a blessing, don't you think? Working so hard to raise money to help people like me and my store?" She glanced up at him, and he tried not to puff his chest out at the description.

Mrs. Swift eyed him, but wouldn't contradict Megan's words. "Did you want to take those items with you now?"

Adam nodded vigorously. "If you have them now, that would be great." Adam doubted he could come in and face Mrs. Swift again.

She sniffed at him a second time then shifted her gaze to Megan. "I'll get them ready."

She left the front of the store to walk into the back. Adam waited until she was gone before he turned to Megan. "What are you doing?"

"I'm not going to let her get away with snubbing the fund-raiser because of your involvement. She can't treat you like that."

"You did until yesterday."

"I did not." She took one of the pastry boxes from him and placed it on the counter near the cash register. "I was…confused and lost in my own pain." She looked up at him. "But things have changed since we talked about Kenny."

He gave a nod. He'd noticed the change in her ever since she'd laid down that heavy burden she'd been carrying around. She was more likely to talk to him, smile at him. He enjoyed the change. "I'm glad things are better between us."

"Me, too." She put her free hand in the crook of his arm and gave him a smile that warmed him from the tips of his toes to the top of his head.

Mrs. Swift returned with three envelopes and a boxed set of Jane Austen novels. "I figured that if I was going to give two gift certificates, I might as well include a third."

"Thank you, Mrs. Swift." Megan patted the pastry box. "Here are some pastries for you and your book club. If you need any more, you let me know."

The sour look on Mrs. Swift's face changed to a soft smile. "That is very generous of you, Megan. Your grandmother

Adelaide would be proud of the young woman you've become."

Megan nodded, then took the books and gift certificates. "That's the best compliment you could have given me. Thank you."

"You have a big legacy to live up to, dear. Don't let her down by the company you keep."

"I am selective with my friends, Mrs. Swift. And Adam couldn't be a better one."

Adam looked at her. He didn't need Megan to defend him to the town, but she seemed more than ready if called on. The look in her eye reminded him of how she'd stood up for Kenny, and Adam wasn't sure if he admired her for rushing to defend him or regretting the need for it. Mrs. Swift, on the other hand, didn't look convinced and gave Adam the eye, then turned and left them standing there.

Without waiting for Megan to follow him, he hustled out of the bookstore and paused to look up and down Main Street. The town hadn't changed much in the years he'd been away while at military school and then college followed by building his career. Much of the same businesses, same citizens and same attitudes. He had run as far as he could from Lake Mildred, but the town wouldn't forget or forgive him.

The bookstore door opened, and Megan came up next to him. She pulled the hood of her coat tighter around her head as a wind started to blow from the north, bringing the smell of imminent snow. She shivered and folded her arms across her chest. "I figure we can probably hit one or two more places before the snow starts."

Adam handed her the pastry box. "I'm done."

She frowned at him but took the box. "We're just getting started. And I'd say we're pretty successful so far." She held up the bag that held the books and gift certificates. "Two stops and two generous donations. Let's not lose our momentum, Adam."

"Why is it such a walk in the park for you? Why do people give you what you want? How did you get such a good reputation in town while I can't live down my past?"

Megan laughed and shook her head. "I've played the good girl for twelve years while you've been gone for the same." She looked up and down Main Street much like he had moments before. "We'll visit the diner next. Rick is a big contributor to the community."

She left him and walked across the street. Adam stared after her. Was this woman for real?

AFTER VISITING THE diner and getting not only promises of donations from Rick but from several of the customers eating dinner there, they stopped at Roxy's department store and talked to the manager, who promised to forward their donation request to the owner. Satisfied with their results, Megs walked back to Adam's truck. She waited while he put Mrs. Swift's donations in the back of the truck, then walked up to help her inside. Before she shut the door, she reached out and put a mittened hand on Adam's cheek. "Hey, we're making progress."

Adam put his hand on hers and removed it from his cheek. She cursed her impulse to touch him, breaking her own rules. She put her hands in her lap while he closed the passenger door and walked around the truck to get in on the other side. He started the engine, then turned in the seat to look at her. "Megan, I appreciate you trying to make inroads for me in the community."

She shrugged it off. "Maybe you deserve a second chance."

"Maybe?" He raised one eyebrow at this, then cracked a smile.

"After what you told me, I gave it a lot of thought and discovered that you really have changed from that bully I remember. You've become a good man."

"Don't glamorize it. I'm far from good. But I am a work in progress." He put the truck in gear and pulled away from the curb, driving toward the bank.

"You're working diligently to make up for how you used to act. Isn't that what a good man would do?"

Adam didn't say anything, didn't even look in her direction. Instead, he concentrated on the road before them as snowflakes started to drift down from the sky. He turned on the windshield wipers to bat them away.

She didn't understand his attitude. He'd tried so hard to convince her he'd changed, but now he wanted to claim otherwise? "Adam, why are you being so rough on yourself? You returned here purposely to make a change in the community. So people aren't exactly flocking to your bank to take you up on your offer for help. Give them time."

He still didn't say anything, but kept his gaze on the road before them. She sighed. "Okay, so it's not as if we have a lot of time on our side with rebuilding going on and the fund-raiser happening next month, but you have to give them a chance. I mean, isn't that what you're asking from them?"

He pulled into the bank's parking lot and stopped next to her car. "Megan..."

"Why don't you call me Megs like everybody else?"

He frowned and stared at her. "What?"

"You always call me by my proper name."

"Because that's who you are." He ran a hand through his hair. "I appreciate you standing up for me with all the Mrs. Swifts in town, but there are some battles I need to fight on my own."

"You mean like Kenny."

"Not everything that happens between us goes back to him."

"Doesn't it?" She gathered her purse and glanced outside to her car next to them. "The snow's really coming down, so I should get home. Good night, Adam. Feel free to finish the pastries that are left."

She hopped down from the truck and slammed the door before he could say anything else. So much for the two of them making progress on their... Friendship? Partnership? Whatever ship it was, it had sailed.

TWO DAYS HAD passed since Megan had stormed out of his truck. Forty-eight hours in which he'd regretted the way he'd shut down on her. They'd forged a peace between them before that, but it seemed to have disappeared, much like she had.

He'd called and left a message asking if she wanted to accompany him to some other businesses. She'd never called him back. He'd texted her to ask how the talent show was coming, but she'd ignored those, too. He only had himself to blame.

It hurt that people wouldn't give him another look once they saw him coming into their businesses or saw his number on their phone. They turned their backs on him. And he wanted to do the same to them if only he didn't need them so much.

He needed this town to forgive him. To allow him to make amends for his past. Because then he could prove he truly was a changed man. Until then, it felt like posturing, that he was just going through the motions. Unfortunately, the townspeople's memories were long and unflinching.

But if Megan could forgive him, couldn't they?

A big if. He doubted she was thinking so fondly of him these past few days. So maybe the town wouldn't forgive him anyway.

He directed his attention back to the theater seat he'd been reupholstering. He would nail a finger to the seat if he wasn't more careful. He finished replacing the red velvet covering, then stood and stretched. Stooping down put too much stress on his back.

"Looks good." Bryan called out to him

as he walked up the aisle. "One down, only about two hundred more to go."

Adam groaned but nodded. He'd promised to help if they could use the theater, and he no longer reneged on his promises when they got too difficult. He took a swig from the bottle of water he'd brought with him. "So why did you buy this place? You're not from around here."

"My Texas accent stand out that much?" Bryan chuckled as he glanced around the theater. "My sister moved up here when she got married. I came for one visit, and I was hooked. I started looking for business opportunities and met this old lady." He put a hand on one of the seats. "Love at first sight. The only way I can describe it."

"It's a run-down theater."

"It's a place of dreams." Bryan patted him on the back. "Now let's get this lady into shape. I want her to be beautiful again."

Adam took another drink of water then wiped his mouth with the back of his hand. "You should have seen this place when I was a kid. They showed cartoons on Saturday for a dollar." He crouched beside the next seat and searched it for any rips or stains. "I spent a lot of my childhood here."

"I love a lady with history." Bryan worked on the row next to Adam's. "Speaking of ladies, where is the lovely one you were with? You two an item?"

Yeah, right. Only in his dreams. "Friends. And working on the fund-raiser together, of course."

"Hmm." Bryan moved on to the next seat and pushed on the back, which made a nasty wrenching noise.

"What does that mean? Hmm?"

Bryan stood and removed the seat back from its spot on the floor. He examined it, then walked it to the aisle where they'd been stacking those that needed more than just their seat covers replaced. He moved to the next seat and used a knife to remove the old velvet fabric from the cushion. "Didn't mean nothing."

"Because there's nothing going on with us. We have history. That's all."

"Old girlfriend?"

Adam shook his head. "Not quite."

"Just that I sensed something going on between you two when you were here the other night." A new piece of velvet in hand, he nailed it into place. "But I've been wrong before."

"You don't know me."

Bryan stood after finishing with the seat. "Sure don't. But take some advice, if you want. A woman like that, she's not likely to stay single for long."

Adam had been wondering why no man had snatched her up before now. She may have devoted her life to her grandmother's bakery, but she had to have a social life, right? She had to have dated in the past. So where was this boyfriend now? Why wasn't she with someone?

Bryan moved to the next seat while Adam remained on his, lost in thought. Maybe she did have someone. Maybe there was a guy waiting for her at the end of the day. Not that he'd seen any sign of one before now. He shook his head. Why was he obsessing over someone who wouldn't return his calls or texts? Was it the chase?

"I didn't mean to get you all up and bothered. Now, are we fixing seats or not?" Bryan moved to the last seat in his row.

Adam glanced at those he still had to reupholster. He stood and pushed his thumbs into the small of his back. “I need a minute, then I’ll be back to work.”

“I’d call her, too, if I were you.”

Adam ignored the other man’s chuckle as he pulled his cell phone out of his jeans pocket and walked up the aisle to the back of the theater. He dialed Megan’s number and waited, but her voice mail answered. He considered hanging up; after all, he didn’t need the drama or headache. He could keep things professional between them. But the beep sounded, and he found he couldn’t. “Megan, I hate how we left things the other night. We were just starting to become friends, and I messed it all up. Please call me.”

When he returned to the seats, Bryan had started working on the row behind him already. Adam knelt down at the last seat he’d been repairing and sighed. Work now. And he’d figure out what to do with Megan later.

MEGS GLANCED AT her cell phone when it buzzed. Adam again. She put it on the couch next to her and flipped the page of the cookbook she'd been absorbed in. Her phone buzzed again. She picked it up and glanced at the screen. He'd left a voice mail.

Not that he hadn't been doing the same thing for the past two days. But she needed space to figure out what had gone wrong. They'd been getting along so well until she'd tried to defend him.

Were male egos really that insecure? They couldn't handle a woman standing up for them, even if that woman was right? She shook her head and placed the phone back on the sofa. She wasn't going to listen to what was probably a repeat of what he'd left before.

Kelly came into the living room and plopped onto the recliner closest to the fireplace where Megs had laid a fire. "I'm bored."

"Because Sam is busy working and we're not?"

"Something like that. He said he'd let me help, but now he says he's not ready for me until the bakery's more safe." Kelly picked up the television remote and started flipping through channels. "Who called you?"

"Nobody."

"The same nobody who's been calling you the past two days?" Kelly lowered the volume on the television and leaned forward, her elbows on her knees. "I thought you said the two of you worked things out."

"We did. But then it stopped." She dog-eared the page she'd been perusing. She could whip up a similar cookie with ingredients she had on hand and make it more commercial. She looked up at her sister. "It's complicated."

Kelly leaned back on the recliner. She pushed the bar to move the footrest up and pulled the quilt Grammy had made over her. "Do you like him?"

"Like him as a boyfriend?"

"I meant as a friend first, but we could go with your first thought of him."

"I don't think of him as a boyfriend. We're barely speaking to each other." She turned another page and huffed when she looked up to find Kelly staring at her, a smirk on her face. "I may have forgiven him, but that doesn't mean I'm in love with him."

Kelly held up her hands. "We're already to love? This is better than a country song."

"I said I wasn't in love. Oh, never mind." Megs picked up her cookbook and walked out of the room.

Kelly followed her to the kitchen. "Can't stand the heat so you come to the kitchen?"

"I'm in the mood to bake."

"And not to talk. I get it." Kelly took a seat at one of the stools at the kitchen island. She rested her cheek on her fist. "You rarely talked about what happened between you two in high school. I remember he was a big bully before his dad shipped him off to military school. Did I miss something? Was there something between you two?"

Only Kenny. Megs shook her head as she pulled flour, sugar and cocoa from the cupboards. "It wasn't like that." She found her chrome mixing bowls and chose the largest. She measured the dry ingredients then retrieved the cream and eggs from the refrigerator. "Is it wrong to speak up for someone? I mean, if they're just standing there, not saying anything, is it okay to step in and defend them?" She placed her items on the counter and took out an egg. She considered it for a moment. "Is there some rule that says you can't?"

Kelly whistled. “Wait. You stuck up for Adam?”

Megs cracked the egg into the bowl and searched for her wooden spoon to mix it into the dough. “And he got upset that I did.”

“Wow.”

“I know. I hated the way that people were judging him, as if they hadn’t been guilty of anything in their lives. He’s not the same boy he was when he left Lake Mildred.” Megs stopped mixing to find Kelly watching her with an odd expression. “What?”

“You are in love with him.”

Megs cracked another egg into the bowl and chuckled as she vigorously stirred the ingredients together. “No.”

“I was teasing before, but you really do love him.” Kelly stuck her finger into the dough and pulled out a dollop. She tasted it then said, “Oh, that’s good.”

Megs pulled the bowl away from her sister’s prying fingers. “Thanks. But you’re wrong.”

“No, it really is good.”

Megs rolled her eyes as she turned to preheat the oven. “I meant about Adam.”

"How many men do you go around defending to the town? That's a pretty bold move to do for someone who's just a friend."

And yet, she'd done that for Kenny, too. Irony was she now defended his bully. "Listen, I'm not sure he's even that." She dropped the dough out onto the counter and started to roll it with her pin. She loved turning a mound of dough into a smooth surface. It gave her a blank slate with which to create a masterpiece. Once she was finished rolling out the dough, she got Grammy's set of cookie cutters. She searched through the tin until she found the desired shape: a diamond. She greased her cookie sheets, then started cutting diamonds from the dough and placing them on the sheet, ready to be baked. Once one tray was full, she looked up at her sister. "I'm confused about how I feel about him."

"So stop avoiding him and talk to him."

She shook her head and worked to fill the next cookie sheet with more diamonds. Once both trays were full, she checked the oven and placed them inside to bake. She set the timer and walked to the refrigerator again, pulling out a carton of fresh blueberries. She poured them into a smaller bowl and mashed them with a fork, then mixed in cream and confectioner's sugar to make a glaze. Kelly reached over and stilled her hand. "Would loving him be so wrong?"

"You have no idea." Sure, she could become friends with him, but anything more would feel like a betrayal to Kenny. She paused from her mixing. And if that was true, then that meant she hadn't forgiven Adam. Not really. She closed her eyes and let out a puff of air. "I guess there are things I still need to work through."

"Okay, but in the meantime, you might be missing out on something great." Kelly swiped her finger through the blueberry glaze. "That's all I'm saying."

ADAM RESTED HIS head against the wall behind him. He'd shed his flannel shirt a while ago and now shivered in his T-shirt. Who knew that reupholstering seats would make him sweat? He let his eyes drift close, but they popped open when his phone pinged. He fished it out of his jeans pocket and read the display.

I don't like how we left things either. But I don't know how to move forward.

His eyebrows raised at this. Interesting. She seemed as clueless as he was about whatever it was between them. Plans tonight? Maybe we could talk.

He sent the message and waited. He didn't realize he was holding his breath until the reply came, and he gasped for air. I know the perfect place to talk. Pick me up at eight?

C U then.

He'd just made a date with Megan Sweet. He couldn't stop the smile forming on his lips.

MEGS WALKED DOWN the stairs a little before eight and paused in front of the hall mirror. She put a hand on her stomach and stared. She wore a blue sweater and jeans, but she still looked as if she was trying too hard. Maybe she should go back up and change.

"Don't you dare," Kelly warned from the

living room. She looked up from the magazine she'd been reading. "You look fine."

Megs walked into the living room and sat on the sofa beside her sister. "I thought you and Sam had plans tonight."

Kelly shrugged. "He's tied up at the bakery longer than he planned. We'll stay in and watch a movie or something if he doesn't fall asleep first."

"He's working too hard."

"He's doing it for you." Kelly put an arm around her shoulders. "For us."

Megs started tapping her foot and glancing at the grandfather clock in the hall. "We're just talking. It's not a date." She reached up and touched her warm cheeks. "So why am I so nervous?"

"When was the last time you went out with a man?" Kelly set her magazine aside. "I haven't seen you date anyone since I came home almost five months ago."

"Dating is overrated. And I told you, this isn't a date." She reached up and patted her hair. She'd tried for casual with a ponytail, but she pulled out the tie and let her hair fall loose around her shoulders. "And I've gone out. Granted, it was over a year ago.

And it wasn't exactly a great time. I had more fun at my last visit at the dentist than I did with him." Headlights glowed from the driveway. Megs stood and put a hand on her belly. "This isn't a date."

"So where are you going?"

"I thought I'd suggest The Vineyard. It's quiet."

"And romantic."

Megs rolled her eyes. That wasn't the goal for tonight. It wasn't even on the radar. "We need a place to talk where we won't be surrounded by people we know."

The doorbell rang, and Kelly rushed forward. "I'll get the door while you take some deep breaths. You look as if you're going to pass out."

Kelly answered the door and smiled up at Adam. "Hi. You look good tonight."

His dark hair appeared damp and recently combed. He wore a navy sweater and jeans, too, but they looked expensive and fit him perfectly. Megs had to admit that he did look pretty good. She stepped forward and grabbed her coat, then turned to her sister. "I won't be late."

Adam took her elbow as they walked

out the door and down the front steps to his truck. He helped her into the passenger seat, his hand lingering longer than usual on her arm before he stepped back and shut the door.

Megs closed her eyes. This wasn't a date. It couldn't be.

Adam got in the truck and pulled out of the driveway. "Where to?"

"The Vineyard." He turned to her, and she was grateful for the darkened car so that he wouldn't see her blush. "I could have said the Penalty Box, but the bar is pretty loud on a Saturday night and full of people who will be speculating what we're doing together. The Vineyard will be a lot less crowded."

"Afraid to be seen with me?"

"That's not what I mean. But there's things we need to talk about and not have a bar full of ears and tongues."

"And you think going to a place the next town over means that no one will find out?" He chuckled. "You have more faith in people than I do. Because I think no matter where we go, there's going to be someone who sees."

"And would it be so wrong if they did?"

"No." He reached over and put a hand over hers. "Relax. We're just talking."

Exactly. At least they were on the same page there.

After a tense and silent fifteen minute drive, Adam pulled into the parking lot of the charming bistro that featured wines from local vineyards. He paused before turning the truck off, turning to her. "And for the record, I'm not ashamed to be seen with you, either."

Inside the restaurant, they were led to a spot near the center of the room. There were tablecloths and cloth napkins, and the wineglasses were made of fine crystal. A fireplace had a roaring fire inside, heating the room and making shadows flicker in the dim lighting. Megs had to hand it to the owners for creating an idyllic intimate atmosphere. Now she wondered if she should have suggested The Penalty Box after all.

Adam perused the menu. "I don't know about you, but I'm starving. Bryan is a strict taskmaster on getting the theater ready for our fund-raiser."

Megs put her menu down. "You've been

working there all day? If you're tired, we could have met another night."

"I finally got you to answer me, Megan. I wasn't going to take the risk of losing out on this opportunity." He gave her a wink and returned to the menu.

Once their dinners and bottle of wine were ordered, tension had returned between them. Megs fiddled with her silverware, unsure of what to say. She knew they needed to talk, but where to start? And how?

"Not everything between us is about Kenny."

Well, that was one way to begin. Megs put her hands in her lap to stop from fidgeting. "Maybe not. But he's still there between us."

"I thought we talked all that out."

"We started the conversation, but there's a lot more to say."

The waitress arrived with their salads. Once she left, Adam shook his head. "The day Kenny died, both our worlds changed. I vowed that I would deal with my anger and learn to become a man others could be proud of. That I could be proud of."

"And yet you still stole a car and got sent to military school."

"Okay, so it didn't happen right that moment. I had some other issues to work out, but I finally got to that point." He picked up his fork and stabbed at his salad. "I vowed that I would never be like my dad. Never use my words to hurt anyone again."

"Has it worked out for you?"

He gave a nod. "What about you?"

"I became a good girl. Someone who follows the rules so that no one would get hurt." She laid the napkin in her lap and smoothed it out. "That's why I like recipes. You follow the directions, and you end up with the perfect dessert. I thought I could apply that to my life, too. Do what is right and find the perfect job, family, everything."

"And has it worked out for you?"

She played with her fork, unable to look at him. Not really, and she didn't know why. She'd done what a person was supposed to do to have a good life: found a job she was passionate about, surrounded herself with loyal family and friends, but she still felt as if she had missed out on something. "Maybe I followed the wrong recipe."

Adam reached out and took her hand in his. "The bakery will be better than it was. I know it. And you'll be successful again."

"But will that make me happy if it didn't before?"

He ran a thumb over her hand. "Yes. Once you let go of the guilt that has hounded you, yes, you'll be happy."

Tears formed in her eyes, and she removed her hand from his embrace. "It's not that easy to let it go."

"I know. It becomes almost like a friend, one you're familiar and comfortable with. But you've got to let it go."

"How?" Megs wiped under her eyes. "I still lost my friend." She let her head fall forward, her grief making it feel heavy. "I can say I'm sorry for my role in what happened, but it won't bring him back."

Adam rose from his chair and knelt beside her. "No, it won't. But neither will wallowing in guilt and acting a victim."

"Is that what I've been doing?"

"I'm not sure, I haven't seen you in a long time, but it appears so." He reached up and put a hand on her cheek, forcing her to look at him. "I'm not saying that there aren't times when I still let it get to me. I'll find myself enjoying something and then think I don't deserve it because of what I did. But Kenny's life won't change if I stay miserable."

"I'm not miserable."

"We can do more for his memory if we live a happy life."

The waitress appeared with their bottle of merlot. She looked surprised to see Adam on his knees in front of Megs, but didn't say a word as she poured the wine in their glasses and left them again. Adam stood and returned to his chair. "Now, I don't know about you, but I plan on enjoying dinner."

He put his napkin in his lap and took a bite of his salad. Megs smoothed the napkin on her lap and followed suit, picking up her fork again. She pushed a few leaves of lettuce around the plate until she chose one and lifted it to her mouth.

Could it really be that simple? Let go of the guilt and enjoy her life? She took a bite and closed her eyes, letting the tangy sensations of the citrus vinaigrette play on her tongue. She could appreciate her life without tarnishing Kenny's memory. But to pursue something more than friendship with the man who had been his tormentor? She didn't know if she could justify that.

AFTER HER SHOW of tears, Megan seemed to relax a little. For that, Adam appreciated the peace that descended on their dinner table. The tension had been thick enough to see it floating in the air until that point. He wondered if the ghost of Kenny would ever depart from between them.

He took a sip of the wine. "This was a good place for us to talk."

Megan looked up from her dinner and shrugged. "I've actually never been here, only heard about it from my customers, who raved about it. They also said I had to try their chocolate mousse for dessert."

"Sounds like a plan. One mousse, two spoons." He gave her a wink.

She frowned a little and clasped her wine goblet tighter. "The roofing company will be working on my bakery starting Monday morning. Things are really coming together."

Okay, so she wanted to change the topic and focus on business. He'd done enough of that to know the drill. "I got word on Friday that the process on your loan is pushing forward faster than first anticipated. We might get a clear to close on it within a week or so. Or at least that's what I'm hoping."

"That is good news. Once the roof is repaired, Sam can begin the restoration of the inside." She dragged her fork about her plate, making trails through the mashed potatoes. "We're hoping for a grand reopening in time for Easter. I really need to get back to work."

"Having free time doesn't agree with you?"

"Too much of it doesn't." She picked up her wine goblet once more but didn't drink. "I'm a 'work first, play later' kind of girl. Probably due to Grammy's influence. I don't know how to relax."

He could see that about her, had probably known it back when they were in high school. She wasn't the kind of person who took things lightly or casually. He'd better remember that if he wanted to pursue something with her.

And he did want to. Her avoidance of him the past few days had only shown him how much he longed to have her be a part of his life. Not for sometimes, but for every day.

After dinner had been eaten, the waitress brought their mousse and two spoons. Adam took a spoonful and held it aloft. "I'd like to make a toast. To the both of us learning to enjoy our lives and letting go of the shackles of the past."

Megan clinked her spoon on his, then took a bite of the mousse. She closed her eyes and moaned. "This is amazing."

He tasted it, too, and found it good, but then he wasn't much of a chocolate person. Still, he liked how much Megan enjoyed it, taking larger spoonfuls and humming her pleasure. He pushed the pedestal bowl closer to her. "Here. You finish it."

"I couldn't." But she pulled the bowl closer and ate the rest of it. Once it was gone, she pushed back her chair from the table. "Now, that was enjoying my life for once."

He smiled at her. “I’m glad you liked it.”

The waitress brought the bill, and Adam gave her his credit card. Megan tried to call her back. She turned to him. “I invited you, so it’s my treat.”

“You can get it the next time.”

“There’s going to be a next time?” Her eyes got wide.

“If you want, there to be one.”

Once the bill was paid and signed for, Adam helped Megan into her coat and put her hand in the crook of his elbow. He walked her to the passenger door of his truck, but didn’t immediately open it for her. When she faced him, he put his fingers to her chin to lift it before he placed a soft kiss on her mouth.

She tasted like red wine and chocolate mousse, an intoxicating combination that made him want to kiss her more. But she took a step back and broke the contact. “This isn’t a date.”

“Wasn’t it? I picked you up. We had dinner and conversation. Now I’ll drive you home and hope for another kiss.”

She hung her head, shaking it from side

to side. “I can’t let this be a date, Adam. Not now. Not ever.”

“Because you won’t let go of Kenny.”

She lifted her eyes to meet his. “Because I don’t have those kinds of feelings for you. Or is your ego too big to handle that?”

“You do have those feelings, but you don’t want them. There’s a difference.” He opened the passenger door and helped her inside before stalking to the driver’s side. He paused before getting in the truck. He wasn’t wrong about her. He could see that she felt something for him even though it hurt her.

They drove back to her house in silence. He’d even turned the radio off, not wanting it to interfere with his thoughts about the woman next to him. He’d admired her since high school. Envied the easy way she had with the townspeople, who clearly loved her. He even thought he might love her if they could get beyond their shared history. But he wasn’t going to beg her to give him a chance. He’d done enough of that with the rest of the town.

He pulled into her driveway and parked behind her sister’s truck. He started to get out, but she opened the door and hopped down before he had the chance. "Thank you for dinner."

Then she was running up the porch stairs and inside the house. He waited for a moment, wishing the night had ended differently before putting the truck into Reverse and heading home to his empty apartment.

MONDAY MORNINGS REQUIRED three cups of coffee to function, but with a surprise visit from his district manager, Adam poured himself a fourth cup. He brought that and one for Dave back to his office, where the other man was perusing Adam's files. He looked up from the report, then nodded and returned his gaze to the paper.

Adam took a seat across from him in one of the chairs normally reserved for his clients and sipped his coffee. He'd been anticipating a visit from Dave, but had hoped it would be later in the week when he had at least half of the six approved loans on the books. As it was, he'd only closed on two of them with an appointment for another on Wednesday, and a fourth would sign by Friday. He had enough in his pipeline that would please his boss, but he'd been hoping for more by now. He really needed to go and visit Shane again. Perhaps he could take Megan with him to convince the man that he needed his help.

Dave cleared his throat, and Adam focused his thoughts on the here and now.

"As you can see, participation in the community fund..."

Dave held up a finger, and Adam stopped talking. He took a sip of his coffee to mask any anxiety. Dave pushed the sheet of paper across the desk. "You've got a good start on the sales numbers that I'm expecting for this branch. But that's all it is right now, a start."

"Yes, sir. And if you look in the second column, we have a quarter of a million dollars in personal and business loans that should close within the next thirty days."

Dave gave a wry smile. "Like I said, it's a start." He rose to his feet, and Adam stood, as well. "You've changed the momentum that the previous manager hadn't been able to, since balances are increasing in the right direction. But I'm hoping to see a bigger jump in deposits by my next visit."

"You will, sir." Adam shook the other man's hand then turned to open the office door. "I think you'll be impressed by the quarterly meeting in April."

"I better be."

Dave started to walk away, then stopped short. Megan stood with a pastry box in her hand. She glanced behind the district manager to Adam. "I'm sorry. I didn't know you had a meeting."

Dave held out his hand to Megan. "I'm Dave Thompson, Adam's supervising manager."

"Megan Sweet of the Sweetheart bakery."

"Ah, yes. Adam's been keeping me updated on the progress of your loan." He glanced at the pastry box. "Did you bring some of your wares?"

Megan opened the box and offered Dave one of the diamond-shaped cookies. "It's a new recipe I've been working on. You'll have to let me know what you think."

Dave took a bite and nodded. "These are fantastic." He turned to Adam. "This woman deserves that loan approved so she can get back to work." He took another bite and nodded. "Absolutely fantastic."

"Thank you, sir."

"That's why working with the community is so important, Dave."

"I can see that." Dave finished the cookie and licked his fingers before grabbing another. "Delicious."

She held out the box for Adam to take one, but he waved her off. He'd wait until Dave left before indulging. Dave clapped Adam on the back, then walked to the teller line to talk to Eva. Megan turned to Adam. "I'm sorry if I interrupted anything."

"Actually, you helped." Adam waved as Dave exited the bank. "Did we have a meeting this morning?"

Megan shook her head. "I wanted to stop by and bring your staff more cookies."

Adam watched her, doubting that was all her visit meant. After all, she could have given Eva the box of cookies and left without stopping by his office. Finally, she shrugged. "And maybe I wanted to apologize for Saturday night."

"What do you have to apologize for? We had a lovely dinner together."

"Until I ran off. I shouldn't have gotten upset after you kissed me."

Adam looked around the lobby to see if anyone had overheard. He ushered Megan into his office and closed the door. "If anyone should apologize for the kiss, it should be me. You clearly weren't ready."

"The thing is I don't know if I'll ever be." She took a seat and placed the pastry box on his desk. "I can see us being friends. You've done a lot to overcome your past, and I'm letting go of my guilt over Kenny, at least, I hope I am, but I can't pursue a relationship with you. It wouldn't be right."

Adam took a seat on the edge of his desk. He'd been afraid she'd say something like that. After dropping her off after their dinner, he'd done nothing but think about her. About how he could have done things differently so he wouldn't scare her away. About what it might take to convince her that they deserved a shot. Now with her sitting before him, all his arguments fled his mind and he was left with questions. "Why not?"

"Because we need to keep what we have professional. You're working on my loan.

We have the fund-raiser we're in charge of. There's too much other stuff going on that I think anything more would be a mistake."

"A mistake?" He let the word bounce around in his mind. Nothing with Megan could be a mistake. "Or maybe the real reason is you're afraid."

"And why shouldn't I be?" She sprung to her feet so that her eyes were on the same level as his. "I can't risk being in a relationship with you."

"Because of my past? My reputation?" He faltered at first, but pushed on. "Don't say it's because of Kenny."

"I don't have to explain myself to you." She pushed her purse strap higher on her shoulder. "We're friends and that's all."

Adam blocked her escape from his office by standing in front of the door. "We're not done here."

"Oh, yes we are." Anger flashed in her eyes. "Now, move away from there."

"Not until you listen to me." He pointed to the chair. "I listened to you, so now it's your turn to hear the reasons why we should be more than friends."

Megan frowned, but took a seat. "Fine."

Adam moved past her and took a seat in the chair next to hers. He held one of her hands and covered it with his. "Megan, you're one of the best people I've ever known. So sweet and kind. Forgiving." Her eyes faltered at this, and she glanced away from him. He clasped her chin and moved her head to look back at him. "I'm…more like a work in progress. But I know that the two of us were brought together for a reason beyond Kenny."

"What reason?"

"I'm not sure yet." He caressed her cheek, reveling in its softness and warmth. "But I won't walk away from something just because I'm afraid, too."

"What are you afraid of?"

"I'd rather die than ever hurt you."

Megan bit her lip and glanced down. He dropped his hands from her face and sat back, giving her space. She finally looked up at him, tears glistening in those beautiful brown eyes. "I'm sorry. But I can't."

And she fled his office.

MEGS GRABBED THE hard hat from her car and headed for the back door of the bakery.

She could see construction workers on the roof already, but she was more interested in what was going on inside. She opened the door and stepped into what would once again be her kitchen someday. Sam had cleared all the debris and had reconstructed the separating wall from the front room. She'd been able to save some of the larger equipment, and she'd been scouring the internet for deals on the rest.

Sam sat on a stool in the front room, perusing the rolled blueprints. A muffled curse from above made him look up, then he spotted her and smiled. "You're not supposed to be here while they're replacing the roof."

"Neither are you." She crossed the room and glanced toward the ceiling. "They give you any idea of how long it will take them to fix my section?"

"Barring any complications, by Wednesday. Then I can get serious in here." He pulled the plans and moved into the kitchen, where he spread the blueprints out and placed coffee cups at the corners to keep them smooth. "I'm starting in the kitchen, since once this is completed, you can begin baking again."

She gave a nod. "I could fulfill my commercial contracts. Bread and rolls for the diner. Cookies for the town council and club meetings."

"It's small, but it's something at least." Sam pointed to the design of the front room. "I had a thought last night about this area. You mentioned the need for a space that could be rented out."

"When I had the loft, it was one thing. I could have rented it out for showers and parties. But now that it's gone, what am I supposed to do?"

"The cost of rebuilding the loft is out of our budget. But we could use a portion of the front room to include a few more tables." He pointed to the spot on the blueprints. "I could build a screen that would divide the front room when in use but fold so that it could be stored. Most of your business is carryout, rather than eat-in, so you wouldn't be sacrificing that much space."

"It's a thought." She closed her eyes, trying to envision it. "And a good one."

Sam smiled at her as he walked her through more of his plans. She agreed with most, but still worried about the cost. That was a thought for later.

When they finished, Sam rolled up the plans and saw Megs to her car. He paused before shutting the door for her, leaning down so he could see her. “I want to ask for your blessing on my marrying your sister.”

Megs switched off the ignition and got out of the car. “You’ve been sitting on this all afternoon and didn’t say anything earlier?”

“I wasn’t sure how to bring it up.” He gave her a grin. “So what do you think?”

Megs squealed and hugged him. “It’s about time. How are you going to ask her?”

Sam grimaced and took a step back. “That’s a good question. It was hard enough asking you for your blessing. I get tongue-tied every time I think about it.”

“It should be special. I mean, it’s a moment that you’ll remember for the rest of your lives.”

Sam swallowed. “Thanks for adding more pressure.”

“That’s what sisters are for.”

WORD HAD REACHED Adam that Megan's loan was ready to close. Underwriting had cleared all questions, so it was only a matter of setting up a time for her and Sam to come in and sign the paperwork. Adam picked up the receiver on the desk phone to call Megan but then replaced it. Maybe news like this was best done in person.

Or maybe he was eager to see her after not hearing a word from her in three days. The town gossip had shared that the work on her roof had been completed, and renovations were progressing on the inside of the bakery. Maybe he'd stop by, hoping she'd be there to share the news. He glanced at his watch. A little early for lunch, but he needed the break.

He chose to walk despite the frigid temperatures. Next to the bakery, he paused outside Shane's aquarium shop. Work had been completed on his roof, too, but the man was still too stubborn to come and ask him for a loan. He lifted his hand to knock on the door but it was gaping open. He heard voices inside.

"He's changed, Shane. You should give him a chance."

He'd recognize Megan's voice anywhere. And she was still defending him, despite the fact that she wouldn't pursue anything more with him.

"Fat chance, you mean. I wouldn't give him the time of day, Megs. And neither should you." Shane's voice. "I remember how he bullied you, too."

"I don't want to stay in my high school days. Do you?" She paused, and Adam leaned forward to try to hear more. "He's really come through for me. And you should go and just talk to him."

"No, thanks."

Adam knocked on the front door. "Megan, I thought I heard you in here. I have good news for you."

Shane scowled at him as he entered the shop. It still looked as if a cyclone had hit. Broken aquariums were stacked against one wall while discarded shelving was pushed against another. It didn't look as though any work besides cleanup had been done yet. Adam glanced around and pulled out his business card. "Seriously, man, you need to come talk to me."

"I told her, and I'll tell you, too. Hell will freeze over first."

"Well, the weather forecast is predicting temperatures below zero, so that might just happen soon. I'm not going to beg."

"And yet, here you are again."

"Because I want to help."

"Help who? To make yourself look good. But you're not really interested in helping out small businesses."

Megan took a step between the two men. She turned to Adam. "You said you had good news for me?"

Adam nodded. "We've gotten the clear to close on your loan. We need to set up a time for you to come in and sign the final paperwork."

"Then I'll get my check?"

"Then you'll get your check."

She turned to Shane. "He could do this for you, too."

The other man waved his hand and walked away. Megan smiled at Adam and let out a loud sigh. "I tried."

"So have I."

"Then, maybe it's time to let it go." She

raised an eyebrow at him. "I've been hearing that a lot lately."

Maybe she was right. He couldn't hound the guy into accepting his help. He'd made the offer and been refused. Time to move on. "It's good advice."

"When do you want to meet to sign the paperwork?" She glanced at her watch. "I'm supposed to see Sam at the bakery this afternoon to go over some plans, then I have a meeting with a dance studio. I thought they might want to be in the talent show, too."

"Tomorrow morning soon enough for you?"

"Perfect." She walked to the front of the store, and he followed her. "Want to see how things are coming next door? Especially since as bank manager you have a professional interest in how well it goes."

Next door, the work showed in so many ways; in particular Adam noticed that Sam had enclosed the kitchen with a shorter ceiling than the soaring one in the front room. He liked how it made the front feel bigger while the kitchen stayed cozy. Megan followed the direction of his eyes. "I can control the humidity and temperature of the kitchen if it's more enclosed. Plus, I have the opportunity to rebuild the loft above the kitchen in the future depending on the success of the Sweetheart."

"I like it." He put a hand against the frame of the wall. It felt solid and reassuring. She was going to get her business and her life back. And he'd made that happen. "It's really coming together for you, Megan."

She gave a soft smile. "With hard work and faith, the Sweetheart will be back and better than before." She stepped away from him and walked through the open doorway to the kitchen area. She ran a hand along the marble counter. "I've missed this place so much." She wiped a tear from her eye. "It was home for a long time."

"I can see why. It's a great place." He looked around the empty kitchen. The silence became uncomfortable. "I should go."

She wiped her face and nodded. "I'll walk you out."

At the door, she opened it but put her hand on his arm. "Thank you for everything you did for me. I really appreciate it."

"You worked hard to get this loan. And I know you'll work just as hard to pay it off." He patted her hand. "Good luck at the dance studio today."

"I'll let you know how it goes."

MEGS PULLED INTO the parking lot of the dance studio and glanced up at it. There had been a time in elementary school when she'd dreamed of becoming a ballerina. She'd begged her parents for lessons, but there hadn't been money for it. And after her dad died and Mom left, Grammy had stepped in, and given all her hard work at the bakery there hadn't been time. If only.

She locked her car and headed inside the two-story building. She could hear a piano playing above her and the thump of shoes on a wooden floor. The woman behind the reception desk looked up at her, and Megs stopped short as a burning sensation formed in her belly and rose up her chest. It was Kenny's mom.

The woman smiled at her. "Megan Sweet? Julie said she had an appointment with you today. Signing up for classes?"

"Mrs. Pierce, you work here?"

"It's Mrs. Jensen now, and I've been the assistant director since, well..." Her voice trailed off, but the smile on her face remained. "I haven't talked to you since you were in high school. How are you?"

Dumbstruck. Terrified. And almost bowed over with guilt. She swallowed, her throat suddenly dry. "Good. You?" Even her voice didn't sound as though it belonged to her. As if she was observing this all happening rather than being an active part of it.

"I was sorry to hear about your bakery. Your honey crullers are my favorite."

"Thank you." She felt as though she was a robot, put on automatic since she didn't know what to say, what to do, what to feel. Kenny's mom acting as if everything was okay. While Megs knew that nothing was. "Is Julie ready for me?"

"Sure." Mrs. Jensen picked up the phone and spoke into the receiver. "Julie says she'll be down in a moment." She looked Megs over. "It's really good to see you. You seem to be doing well."

Megs nodded. "You, too." She took a step away, then turned back. "Mrs. Jensen, I'm really sorry about Kenny."

"I am, too, honey. He was a troubled boy." She let her smile drop for a second, then pasted it back on when Julie walked into the lobby. "Thank you, Megs. Julie will see you now."

Megs followed Julie up to her office past two dance rooms, both with mirrored walls and a long wooden bar running along it. The piano in one of the rooms played a light tune, but the heavy heartbeat inside Megs's chest made it almost difficult to breathe. Once they reached Julie's office, Megs tried to swallow. "I hate to ask, but can I bother you for a drink of water?"

Megs tried to pull herself together while Julie was gone. She took several deep breaths, closing her eyes. She pictured Adam telling her to let it go. But it didn't help. Instead, when Julie returned, Megs thrust a copy of the flyer at her. "I'm sorry, but I'm not feeling well and need to leave. Here's the information we discussed over the phone. Feel free to call me if you have questions."

"Will you be okay to drive home? You're shaking."

Megs nodded, then walked quickly out of the studio, not even glancing at Mrs. Jensen as she left the building. She ran to her car and opened it, then locked herself inside. She tried to catch her breath. Tried to calm the erratic beat of her heart. She needed to talk to someone. But her sister didn't know, wouldn't understand. Only one person would. She grabbed her phone and dialed Adam's number, hoping that he wasn't busy with a customer. She started to cry when he answered.

"Megan? Are you okay?"

She took big gulps of air and shook her head. "No."

"Where are you?"

"The dance studio out by the highway."

"I'll be right there."

She hung up the phone and waited for help to come.

ADAM PULLED INTO the parking lot of the dance studio and found Megan's car parked near the back underneath a willow tree that had ice encasing its leaves, making them droop toward the ground. He shut off his truck and walked to where he found her slumped over the steering wheel, her shoulders shaking. He could hear her heartbreaking cries even through the closed window. She looked up at him and opened the door. She pushed herself into his arms, wrapping hers around his waist and resting her head against his chest. He put one arm around her back while he smoothed her hair with the other. He had no idea what had sparked such grief, but her sobs racked her body and she clung to him. "It's going to be okay."

She sobbed more and took fistfuls of his jacket. "I can't live like this, Adam. I need your help."

He pressed a kiss to the top of her head. "I'll do whatever you need me to do. But you have to tell me what happened."

"Kenny's mom is here. I couldn't look at her." She hiccupped and pressed her face against the front of his jacket. "She treated me so nice. She doesn't know what I did."

Adam put a hand under her chin and pushed her head up so she could look at him. "We should talk to her. Because until you get free of this, you can't move forward."

Her eyes were wide with fear. "I can't talk to Mrs. Jensen. You don't understand. I tried, but I couldn't." She closed her eyes and moaned. "She treated me so…nice. I think that hurt more."

He glanced up at the front door of the dance studio. "I've been wanting to apologize to her for a long time. Maybe this is a sign." He put a hand on Megan's cheek. "For both of us." Megan blinked several times, and he touched her hair, letting the golden strands run through his fingers. "Megan, you don't need to hurt like this anymore. And we'll do it together. Let's ask her to meet us for coffee. And you can bring some dessert."

She gave a short nod. "Can you set it up? I can't see her like this right now."

He helped her into her car, then peered at the dance studio. He walked with purpose to the front door, then opened it and stepped inside. An older woman sat at the reception desk, typing into a computer. She looked up at him, and he stopped cold. She had Kenny's eyes. But he needed to do this. For Kenny. For Megan.

For himself.

He continued on to the desk. "Mrs. Jensen, I don't know if you remember me but I'm—"

"Adam Hawkins. I remember you." She gave him a soft smile. "You're interested in taking lessons?"

"Uh, no. I was wondering if Megan Sweet and I could talk to you some evening."

"Talk about what?"

Adam cleared his throat and glanced at a group of girls chatting as they exited the studio. He turned back to Mrs. Jensen. "Kenny, of course. There's some things I've wanted to say to you for many years." He looked around the studio. "Things to be shared in private."

Mrs. Jensen paused while more girls and boys left their lesson and walked out to the parking lot. She waited until the lobby was again empty. "There are some things I've meant to say to you, too." She glanced at her watch. "Tomorrow evening about seven at my house. Megs knows where it is. It's the same one I've lived in for years."

Adam extended his hand. "Thank you. This means a lot."

Mrs. Jensen stared at his hand while several seconds ticked by. Then she shook it slowly. "Until tomorrow."

Adam returned to Megan's car. She had found tissues and had cleaned up her appearance, although he still found her beautiful. He leaned against the car as she rolled down the window. "We'll meet with her tomorrow night."

Megan stared at the studio. "Are you sure this is the right thing?"

"It's not the easy thing to do, but yes, I think it's the right thing." He leaned down so he could see her face better. "Will you be okay driving home or do you want me to take you?"

She shook her head. "I'll be fine."

"Okay. But I'll follow you to make sure you get home all right."

She started the car, but didn't roll up the window. She ducked her head. "Thank you for meeting me. I didn't know who else to call."

"I'm glad you did."

ADAM FLIPPED THROUGH the pages, making sure that everything in the loan package was ready for their signatures. He glanced at the clock on his computer. Five more minutes.

Why was he so nervous about this loan closing? He'd done about a hundred in his time at the bank, so it was old hat for him. But he'd never had so much riding on one before. Megan's future. And possibly his.

He left the paperwork on his desk and walked out into the lobby. They had a line waiting for the tellers. It was Friday and payday for most of the town employees, so that wasn't unusual. But the line seemed longer. Maybe with more of the accounts being opened at their branch, they'd see more foot traffic. Exactly what Dave wanted.

The door at the end of the hall opened, and Megan stepped inside. She pushed her hood back from her face and smiled when she spotted him. "Am I late?"

He approached her. "Early. Sam hasn't arrived yet." He glanced at her empty hands. "No pastries today?"

"Eva warned me that the staff is gaining weight these days and suggested I limit my offerings." She strode past him and into his office. She took off her coat and placed it on the seat closest to the window and set her purse on top before sitting. She was ready.

So was he. "If you don't mind, we can go over some of the paperwork that wouldn't involve Sam." He pulled his desk chair around so that they could sit side by side while he went over the terms and conditions, pointing out key dates and figures. "If you default on the loan, the bakery could become the property of the bank." He looked up at her. "Not that I'm expecting you to, but I make sure to let my clients know the worst-case scenarios."

"I'm not a worst case." She signed her name at the bottom of the page. "And I'm well aware of the responsibility that I'm taking on with this loan. Grammy taught me the basics of running a business, including paying the bills first."

He nodded and turned to the next page. She read it over and signed where indicated. "You don't need to spell out everything for me. I'm pretty smart on my own."

"I don't want there to be any surprises down the road." He pointed to the next section and discussed the repayment plan and monthly interest. "And of course, if you pay off the loan sooner, you'll pay less in interest down the road."

"Yes, I've got that." She signed her name and glanced at him. "Are you ready for tonight's meeting with Mrs. Jensen?"

He flipped the page and explained how the interest rate was derived until her eyes glazed over. Finally he nodded. "I spent last night preparing how I'm going to apologize to her for all the pain I put her son through."

Megan signed her name with a flourish. "That's more than I've done. I tossed and turned, worried about what she'd say back to me."

"She seems nice."

"Her son is dead, and we played a part in that." She put the pen down on the desk and sat back in the chair. "I can't imagine how she felt that day when she discovered Kenny's body. And what she's felt ever since. Kenny was an only child, so she buried not only her son but all hopes for grandchildren. Then she got divorced."

"And remarried."

"Her life hasn't turned out the way she'd planned."

Adam stacked the pages and reviewed them to make sure every one was signed or initialed. Satisfied, he tapped them on the desk to straighten them, then placed them in the manila folder. "Mine didn't. How about yours?"

"But I didn't lose my son." Megan shifted in her chair. "My stomach is in knots already, and we have hours before we're expected at her house."

"So why don't you do some baking and get your mind off it? Isn't that what you usually do?"

"Not that easy this time. But I can give it a try."

Adam nodded, then put a hand on her cheek. "I wish I could take this pain away from you. Protect you as you should have been before."

Megan swallowed and licked her lips. He let his gaze drop there for a moment, then rise back to her eyes that burned with confusion.

A knock on the door broke up the moment, and Sam stepped inside. Adam dropped his hand, but not before the other man noticed. "Am I interrupting something?"

"No." Megan leaned back in her chair. "Adam's been going over some of the paperwork with me while we waited for you."

"Sorry. I got caught up in installing the new dishwasher." He grinned at Megan. "You've got to stop by and see it before you go home. It's a beaut."

Adam put his professional hat back on and completed the paperwork with both of them. Once they had signed and initialed all pages, he handed Megan the check from the loan proceeds. "I'll pick you up at six thirty."

Sam's eyebrows rose at this, but he stood and didn't say a word. Instead, he shook Adam's hand. "I'll see you at the bakery, Megs?"

She nodded at him. "I have some things to take care of before I can get over there, but I'll be there." Once Sam left, she turned to Adam. "Talking to Kenny's mom, we aren't going to stir up things that are best left buried?"

"I have a feeling that tonight will be cathartic not just for us but Kenny's mom, as well."

AFTER SHE LEFT, he checked to find out if his next appointment had arrived. He surveyed the bank lobby and saw a teenaged kid slouched in one of the chairs. He looked familiar, but Adam couldn't place him. He went over to him. "Are you Keegan Fox?"

The kid glanced up at him, then around the room before giving a nod. "They said you were tied up with someone."

"I'm ready now for you." He swept his arm toward the office and noticed how the kid stood and slunk inside before slumping into a chair. Adam closed the door, then took the seat behind the desk. "Mr. Fox, what brings you into Foster?"

"Listen, I told the lady that I wanted a savings account, but I wanted to talk to you without everybody hearing us." Keegan sat up a little straighter and leaned his elbows on his knees. "I heard that speech you gave about bullying at school. And that we needed to speak up."

Adam nodded. "Are you being bullied?"

Keegan gave a sharp laugh and shook his head. "Hardly. Don't anyone mess with me."

And at once, Adam knew where he recognized the kid. It was himself at that age. Same chip on his shoulder. Same anger and pain in his eyes. "Why did you want to talk to me?"

"Something you said that day stuck with me. About being angry, you know? How did you get rid of it?"

Adam mulled that over. "Anger isn't something you get rid of. Instead, it's something you learn to harness and control." He pulled out his wallet and handed the kid a picture of himself in uniform. "It took being sent to military school to learn how to deal with my anger issues."

The kid looked at it then handed it back to him. "Thanks, but no thanks. I'm not looking to join the army or whatever." He paused and looked down at the floor. "But I need something. I can't keep going this way."

"How are things at home?"

Keegan rolled his eyes. "I thought you were a banker, not a shrink."

"My dad only knew one way to talk to me, and it wasn't nice. And when he didn't think I heard his words, he used his fists. And then my favorite was when he got out his belt." Adam peered at the kid. "Sound familiar?"

"I'm not you."

"Then, why did you come to see me?"

Keegan stood. "You know what? Forget it."

Adam stood, too. "No. You wanted to talk, so let's talk. What's the bad stuff? The stuff that you don't tell anyone. Like how it feels good to make fun of the weak kids. Until later when you realize the words you used are the same ones you hear your dad call you. And then you feel worse. So then you have to go hurt someone else. And you wish that you wouldn't turn into your old man, but it's like fate."

"It's my mom," Keegan whispered.

"Same thing."

Keegan clenched his jaw and glared at Adam. "I gotta go."

"All right." Adam stood aside and opened the door. "But if you need to talk to someone, here's my card." He wrote his cell phone number on the back of it. "You can call me anytime."

The kid walked out with a grunt, and Adam wondered if he'd ever see him again.

MEGS FIDGETED IN the passenger seat, playing with the string on the pastry box. She'd spent most of the afternoon debating what to make for their dessert. She'd ended up making crullers, Mrs. Jensen's favorite. The smell of the sugar and honey filled the cabin of the truck.

Adam reached over and put his hand over hers to still them. "It's going to be okay."

"Or maybe she agreed to meet with us because she's been waiting to scream at us." She took several deep breaths. "But we won't know until we face her."

He pulled into the driveway of Kenny's old house, and Megs gasped. "It looks the same as it did before."

Adam turned to look at her. "Some things don't change." He squeezed her hand. "Are you ready?"

No. She'd never be ready to face Kenny's mother and confess her role in his death. But it had to be done. She took off her seat belt and opened the passenger door. She didn't wait for Adam, but took the leap on her own, landing in a snowdrift. At least she'd worn her boots.

Adam walked around the truck and took

hold of her elbow to lead her up the sidewalk to Mrs. Jensen's house. He opened the screen door and looked at her, but she shook her head so he knocked and waited. A man who must be Mr. Jensen appeared and escorted them in. "Wendy said she had company stopping by. Please come in."

They followed him down the short hall to the kitchen and family room in the back. Mrs. Jensen stood by the sofa and gestured toward the two recliners. "Can I get you two something to drink?"

Megs held up the pastry box. "I brought your favorites."

Mrs. Jensen accepted the gift and walked into the kitchen, where she opened the box and put several on a plate. She returned and offered some to them. Megs shook her head. She couldn't eat. Her stomach threatened to revolt if she tried.

Adam accepted one and took a seat. Megs waited until Mrs. Jensen sat, then took the other recliner. She sat on the edge, her eyes darting around the room. It was the same but different. The television was newer, and so was the other furniture. But the pictures on the wall were the same. She stared up at Kenny's portrait from their freshman year. The last picture he'd had taken.

Adam put his cruller to the side and turned to Mrs. Jensen. "I think you know why we're here."

She gave a nod, her face becoming serious. "I've been waiting for this moment for twelve years."

Adam cleared his throat and leaned forward. "Mrs. Jensen, I bullied your son. Pushed him into a dark place that he couldn't get out of. It's because of the horrible things I said and did that he ended his life." He choked up and dropped his gaze to the floor. "I apologize for everything I said and did to Kenny. I hope that maybe one day you could forgive me."

Mrs. Jensen frowned. "I knew what you did to my son and why. But you're not responsible for his suicide."

"But if I hadn't said those things..." He shook his head. "I told him he'd be better off dead."

"That does sound bad, I'll admit. But it's not your fault."

"It's mine." Megs wrung her hands together. "I should have helped him, but I made it worse."

Mrs. Jensen turned to Megs "Is that the reason you hide in the kitchen when I visit your bakery and you avoid me at the grocery store?" She looked up at Kenny's portrait. "You were his best friend. But it's as if you disappeared after he died."

"Because I couldn't face you. I couldn't save him, and it's all my fault."

Mrs. Jensen reached out and took both of their hands in hers. She looked at Adam. "Maybe if you'd been kinder." She turned to Megs. "And maybe if you'd talked to him that afternoon." She took a deep breath. "Or maybe if I'd come home from work a half hour earlier. There's a lot of maybes that could have altered what happened that day, but we can't change it now." She let go of their hands and walked to the fireplace, her expression calm. "It's taken a lot of years of therapy for me to say that my son was troubled. And he only saw one way out of his pain. That was his choice, to end his life. And we can't go around and assign blame or guilt to everyone and everything." To Megs she said, "It's not your fault. It never was."

Megs stared up at her, tears streaming down her face. Why was Mrs. Jensen letting her off so easy? "But I made the bullying worse for him by standing up to Adam. He blamed me for it."

"It's not your fault." She turned toward Adam. "No more than it's yours. That's why I forgave you long ago."

Adam hung his head, and Megs rose to her feet and sat on the arm of the recliner, her arms around his shoulders. He looked up at Mrs. Jensen. "Thank you."

She took his hand in hers again and squeezed it. "Thank you for finally coming to face me." She put a gentle hand on Megs's arm. "And you, too. We needed to clear the air between us long ago." Mrs. Jensen took a deep breath, then rubbed her hands together. "Now that that is out of the way, how about I make some tea to go with our doughnuts?"

They stayed for more than an hour, then left with promises to see her at the talent show in a few weeks. Megan walked slowly in front of Adam then stopped to look up at him. "What happened in there?"

"We were forgiven." He put his arm around her shoulders and escorted her to the passenger door. "That is the coolest lady I've ever met."

"Why did she do that? Just forgave us without a second thought? I still feel the need to pay some kind of penance."

"I know." His face was only inches from hers; he wanted to kiss her, to absolve her from any sin with such a kiss. But he wasn't the man to do that. He backed away. "That's why we need to live a life that Kenny would be proud of."

"And how do we do that?"

Adam didn't answer. He'd tried to become a good man, giving back to those who needed help. To become someone positive in the community. He'd earned a degree in finance less because of his love of business and more for the opportunities that it gave him to assist others. He'd risen quickly through the ranks of Foster Community Bank because he'd been known as a fair and ethical banker who advocated for the needs of his clients. And yet, he still felt this need to do more, to be more. He was still trying to make up for the sins of his youth.

He drove Megan home, then walked her to her front door. The porch light cast pretty golden sparks in her hair. He nodded at her and took a step down. "Good night."

"Wait." Megan grabbed his arm and pulled him to her. She put her hands on his neck and kissed him on the cheek.

She started to take a step back, but his arms went around her waist and he brought her closer. His mouth descended on hers, and she moaned against his lips. Taking this as encouragement, he deepened the kiss, reveling in the sweet taste of her. Wanting to never leave her side.

The front door opened, and Megan's sister whistled. "Would you two like to come in rather than stand outside in the freezing cold?"

Megan glanced up at him, then brushed past her sister. Adam cleared his throat. "Ms. Sweet, have a good night."

"You bet." She shut the door, and he regretted that he hadn't had more of a chance with Megan.

MEGS TOOK OFF her jacket and hung it up on the rack in the foyer. She touched her blazing cheeks. What had she been thinking? That was the problem. Her brain had short-circuited when Adam had kissed her. She glanced in the hall mirror and sighed. She looked like a woman who had been kissed well.

Kelly clucked her tongue. "I thought you said the two of you were just friends."

"We are." Megs rushed into the kitchen and started to unload the dishwasher. She needed to keep busy and debated trying a new recipe that she'd been considering for the reopening. It was a rustic bread with seeds and nuts. She'd search for the cookbook once the dishwasher was empty.

Kelly wouldn't give up and entered the kitchen, sitting on a stool and watching her put plates away in the cupboard. "How did it go tonight?"

Wonderful. Horrible. She'd been forgiven by Mrs. Jensen, but she didn't feel as if she'd deserved it. "I'll tell you, but first I want to ask you a favor."

"Sure. Anything."

Megs leaned against the counter. "Would

you write me a song? Then maybe perform it with Sam at the fund-raiser?"

"About anything in particular?"

She nodded and shut the dishwasher. "I need to tell you about what happened not just tonight, but twelve years ago."

And she laid it all out. The facts of what happened. Her own culpability and living with the guilt since then. Kelly didn't say a word, but listened, nodding every once in a while. When Megs finished, her sister got off the stool and walked around the kitchen island. She put her arms around her and rested her head on her shoulder. "I can't believe all that happened, and you never told me."

"I couldn't tell anyone. Not even Grammy knew about how guilty I felt. And she knew most of my secrets."

Kelly left her arm around Megs. "I'll write a song with Sam, and we'll perform it at the fund-raiser. I've already got ideas."

"I want to do something to honor Kenny, you know? To make up for what I did."

"What you did was try to help him. It's not your fault that he died."

She was starting to realize that more

now. She'd done what she thought was right. And if she had to live it over again, she'd still stand up for him. Because that was what you did for friends. You stood up for them when they couldn't do it for themselves. And Kenny would never have done it. "I only wish that I could have convinced him that he didn't have to kill himself."

"Did you even know he was thinking about it?"

Not a clue. She'd been just as shocked when the announcement had come over the PA that morning. "No."

Kelly rubbed Megan's back. "I know it's hard to hear, but it seems as though he was determined that this was the only way."

"Mrs. Jensen said the same thing."

"Then, it's probably true."

"I know that in my head, but I've been carrying it around for so long that I don't know how to make the guilt go away." Megs sagged onto a kitchen stool. "How do I convince my heart?"

"Day by day, Litt."

Kelly was playing hardball by dragging out their old nickname. Short for Little since Kelly was shorter, but Megs was younger. "Letting go of something I've held so tightly isn't easy."

"So you loosen your grip a little, just a little, every day until it's been released." She paused then took a deep breath. "Have you thought about seeing a therapist? You know Page would take you on if you wanted someone to talk to."

"I'm talking to you."

"I meant someone professional. What would it hurt?" She put a hand on her shoulder. "And more important, what would it help?"

She hadn't talked about Kenny in twelve years until the past few weeks. Could she allow the floodgates to open, the guilt and the grief? Could she share in what she'd been living with every day, and by sharing release it? She gave a quick nod. "I'll think about it."

CHAPTER SEVEN

WITH WORK PROGRESSING on the bakery and the fund-raiser looming in a week, Megs didn't have much time for thinking and ruminating on her past. In fact, she did little more than confirm acts for the talent show and check on the progress of her new kitchen.

She slapped the hard hat on her head and pushed through the back door of her bakery. In the kitchen, she admired the stainless-steel-door walk-in refrigerator that had been delivered that morning, reveling in its cool smoothness.

"It's just a fridge."

She turned and found Sam smirking at her. She gave him a shrug. "It's more than that. It holds essential ingredients for my business. And it's beautiful."

"So was the price." He handed her the bill of sale. "I was able to negotiate him down another five hundred since I could pick it up myself rather than paying for delivery."

"Nice. Thanks."

"Sure." He led her over to the ovens he'd been able to salvage. "And I fixed the faulty thermometer on the lower oven so now they'll heat evenly."

"You're handy to keep around."

"I'll remind you of that when you see my final bill." He leaned against the marble island. "You ready for the fund-raiser?"

Didn't matter if she was ready, they were only five days away from it. "The bigger question is do you have my song ready?"

"It's good, too. Maybe Kelly and I can play it for you tonight after dinner."

She winced. "I want to hear it for the first time Friday night with everyone else. Bad enough that I've heard snippets of it while Kelly practices."

A knock on the front door. Megs frowned, but went to answer it. Adam stood there. "Did you hear the bad news?" He paused on his way into the front room and looked around. "Sam started work in here."

"He finished the kitchen last week. Come take a look at your investment."

She grabbed his hand and pulled him through the open doorway to the kitchen. Adam whistled. "Nice. Even I would want to bake in here. And I'm a disaster with an oven."

Sam grinned. "She only hires the best."

"I can see that." Adam gestured at the wall she shared with the aquarium shop. "Have you been able to give Shane a hand?"

"As much as he'll let me."

"You said there was bad news?" she asked.

Adam blinked at her several times, then nodded. "Right. They're saying on the radio that we're expected to get at least a foot of snow by the weekend."

"Not during the talent show?"

Adam's mouth formed a grim line. "Afraid so. I've already had two acts call to cancel."

"But without acts, we won't have an audience. And without an audience, we won't have people bidding on the prize packages. Which means…"

"Which means the fund-raiser could be

dead in the water. And after all our hard work. And the kids."

Sam glanced between the two of them then shook his head. "Do you really think something like that is going to stop Lake Mildred from turning up for this event? I may be a fairly new citizen, but even I know that they wouldn't let a few inches of snow stop them."

"It's more than a few inches. It's a foot."

"Foot shmoot." Sam gathered his tool belt and the sander he'd brought in from his truck that morning. "I need to get back to work. And you two need to stop focusing on the negative."

He left them, and a few moments later, the sander started to whine. Adam glanced at Megs. "He's right. Weather forecasters are known for being wrong."

"Right." But she hated to think that all their hard work would leave them without anything to show for their efforts.

"I helped Bryan finish the major repairs of the theater, so it's all set. Three hundred and sixty seats primed for Lake Mildred and its stars." He put a hand on hers. "It's going to be okay."

"I have all the desserts baked and ready. And I have to pick up the programs tomorrow afternoon." She mentally reviewed her list of things to finish before the show. "We will need to set up Thursday night at the theater if you're available."

"Of course."

Megs took a deep breath, feeling the pressure of what they were doing. Not just for herself, but for the many in the community who had been affected. Sure, her business had taken a hit. But in retrospect, it hadn't been a complete disaster for her. Not like it had been for some. She let her eyes drift in the direction of Shane's shop and sighed. "Come on." She grabbed Adam's hand and pulled him out of the back door of the bakery and toward the aquarium shop.

"I've tried with him, Megan. It's no use."

"So try again." She knocked, then opened the back door. "Shane, you in here?"

"Yes." The word sounded so mournful. He poked his head out from behind a large shelving unit. "What is he doing here?"

"You need help, and he's offering it. Now I think it's time for you both to get over it.

Your pride, Shane." She turned to Adam. "And your fear."

Shane scoffed. "What does he have to be afraid of?"

"Your rejection." Adam took a step forward. "A guy can only take so many noes before it becomes a blow to his ego."

"This isn't about your ego."

"No, it's about your shop. Your future." Megs took Adam's hand and tugged him closer to Shane. "You need to accept that Shane is having a hard time letting go. That it might be a while before he forgives you." She took Shane's hand in her free one. "And you need to accept his help without thinking it means that the past didn't happen."

Both men looked at the floor, the walls, anywhere but at each other. Megs sighed. "Fine. I'm out of here. You two need to work this out because this shop won't reopen if you two can't find some kind of compromise." She stormed out.

SHANE GRINNED AFTER Megan's departure. "I always thought she was the nice Sweet sister, but I may have been wrong."

Adam smiled at that. "She can be fierce."

Shane's smile faded. "I don't want your help."

"I know. You've made that very clear."

The other man huffed loudly. "But that doesn't mean I don't need it." He glanced around the store. "This was my whole life, and in a few seconds, it was taken from me."

"It doesn't have to be that way. If you'd get beyond your stubborn pride..."

"If you're trying to butter me up, it's not working." He put his hands on his hips. "If I don't get some kind of assistance, I'll never reopen my doors. And that's not an option I want to accept."

"So why don't you come down to the bank, and we can discuss options?" Adam shrugged, kept his eyes on the chaos surrounding them. "Foster Community has a good reputation of lending responsibly to small businesses like yours, not just loans but with savings and insurance to prevent future losses."

Shane didn't look at him or say a word, but his jaw clenched tighter. Then he sighed. "Why did you do it? We'd been best friends in junior high. Then you shot up in height. And in popularity, and I was old news."

"I was a stupid kid."

Shane looked at him. "You shoved me in my locker at least once a month for four years. You called me names. You threatened me with violence."

"I'm sorry for how I treated you."

"Why should I believe you?"

"Because I'm not that kid anymore." He leaned back against the shelving unit. "Something happened our senior year that made me take a good hard look at the jerk I'd become. And I couldn't face myself in the mirror. I had to change."

"You left town."

He paused, debating how much to share with Shane. Deciding that it wouldn't hurt him now to be completely up front, he continued, "A kid killed himself because of me. Because of the things I called him. By that point, I hated myself so much I would have done anything to prove to the world that I was the bad one. That I had deserved to die, not that kid. I had to do something to get out of this town, so I stole my dad's car knowing it would be the last straw. He sent me away to military school, and I'm grateful he did. They broke the old me and helped me create the man I wanted to be."

"Why are you telling me all this?"

"Because you wanted to know why you should believe me. Well, I'm telling you that words are words, but I've made my life into something to be proud of because I'm ashamed of my past. You can find the proof in the man I am, and by what my clients and friends say of me now."

Shane stared at him. "You'll give me references?"

"I'll do you better. You can have my cell phone and call any five numbers and ask them." He took his phone out of his pants pocket and held it out. "Any five."

The other man paused, the silence in the shop deafening. This was Adam's, and thus Shane's, last chance. Either he believed him or it would never happen. And Adam would move on, stop trying.

Finally Shane nodded. "Okay. But I'll do it without an audience." He took the phone and walked into the other room.

Adam let out a deep breath, then turned and found a chair. *This could take a while.*

After five minutes, Shane returned and held out Adam's phone. "I need to think about it. I can't give you an answer right now."

"Fair enough." Adam glanced at his phone. "Who did you call?"

"Doesn't matter. They all said the same thing."

Shane walked out of the room while Adam pulled up the call history. Only two calls, and the last had been to his own father.

THURSDAY AFTERNOON, MEGS loaded the trunk of her car with all the pastries she'd made for the fund-raiser. Kelly ran out the side door with Sam's guitar case. She put it in the backseat with care, then took the front seat. Megs got in and turned to her sister. "Did we remember everything?"

"The good thing about setting up the night before is you have another day to bring whatever you forgot." She peered up through the windshield at the sky. "The snow's really coming down already."

"Don't remind me." Despite prayers to the opposite, the sky had opened up an hour ago and several inches of fresh snow already coated the ground. Megs hoped that the dire predictions had been exaggerated. She started the car and headed over to the theater.

Bryan had told her he'd leave the side door unlocked for them, so she parked near it so that they could unload her car. She tried the door. Bingo. Unlocked. She propped the door open for easier access then started the arduous task of carrying three dozen full pastry boxes. Once her car was empty, she moved it to the front. Her tire tracks were already covered with fresh snow. Great.

She heard a truck growling and saw Adam making the turn into the parking lot. But he must have misjudged it as he fishtailed into a nearby ditch and struck a tree. Megs gave a shout then ran to the truck. She reached the driver's side and pulled open the door. Adam had a hand on his forehead and his eyes were shut. "Are you okay?" she asked.

He moaned and opened an eye at her. "I think so."

"Should I call for an ambulance?" She

put his arm around her shoulder and put hers around his middle.

"I'm all right."

"Do you think you can walk to the theater?"

"I didn't hit my head that hard." He eased out of the seat and groaned as he put his feet on the ground. "My truck."

"We'll have to call a tow truck to get you out, I think. But I doubt they'll be able to get here tonight. I'll drive you home." She kept talking as they walked in tandem to the theater, her arms around him to support him if he needed it. "Kelly and I got all the desserts inside so that's done. And we only have to set up about six tables in the lobby for the silent auction. And then—"

"Megs."

She looked up at him. "Am I hurting you?"

"You're talking too much." He gave her a lopsided grin. "I think you're worried about me."

"I read in a magazine that you have to keep a person with a concussion awake."

"I don't think I have a concussion. Just a bump."

They made it to the side door, and Megs swung it open and let him enter first. Kelly ran up to them. "I heard the commotion. Are you okay?"

"He claims he's fine." Megs rolled her eyes.

"Maybe we should keep him awake just in case he has a concussion."

"That's what I said."

The two sisters grinned at each other, then turned to Adam, who winced and pointed to a chair at the edge of the stage. "I'll just take a seat over there."

Megs watched him hobble to the chair and moan as he lowered himself into it. He could have injuries that weren't showing, and if the snow kept up at this rate, they'd be stranded in the theater overnight. She glanced at Kelly. "Should we call an ambulance?"

"He said no. He keeps saying he's fine." She peered at him. "But we'll keep an eye on him."

Kelly's phone buzzed, but she ignored it. Megs lifted one eyebrow at this. "You're not going to answer Sam's text?"

"We're having a fight, nothing big."

"But you'll still perform tomorrow night?"

"The show always goes on." Kelly glanced around the theater. "You said Bryan would leave the tables for us to set up. I wonder where they are?"

Megs searched around then walked off the stage and down the center aisle to the lobby. Once there, she noticed that not only had Bryan set up the tables, but he'd draped them in red tablecloths. She smiled and went back into the auditorium. "Found them. Grab the box with the prize clipboards so we can get that set up." She squinted through the dark theater. "How are you doing, Adam?"

"Doing good." He lumbered to his feet and followed Kelly to the lobby. "It looks great in here."

"Bryan really went above and beyond." Megs took the box from Kelly and placed it on one table. "If we push these tables against the walls, we'll still have room in the lobby for people to mill around. Put sports-related prizes on one table. Educational on another. Edible, et cetera."

With Kelly's help, Megs got the tables moved where she wanted them while Adam sorted through the clipboards and put them in categories. He whistled as he saw the stacks of prize packages. "I'd hoped we'd get a decent showing, but people went overboard in their generosity."

Megs shrugged. "Once they realized how important it was, they opened their arms."

"You mean, once you got hold of them they gave you what you wanted." He started to place clipboards on each of the tables. "They had no problem turning me down."

"It wasn't quite like that."

Adam turned to Kelly. "It was exactly like that."

"You two always like this?" Kelly looked at them, a smirk on her face. Her phone buzzed again, and she sighed. "I'll tell him that we're okay."

She tapped out her message, then put her phone back in her pocket. "Sam said the roads are getting really bad. We'd better hurry and finish up here so we can drive home safely."

They finished placing the clipboards out, then walked back into the auditorium. Megs stopped to notice the red velvet seats. "I can't believe you got the place looking this fantastic in time for the show."

"I only helped. Bryan was the powerhouse on this project."

She put a hand on his arm. "Thank you for all your hard work."

"You did the hard part. Calling and getting all those donations. And the acts for the show? That was you."

"Actually, my sister did a lot of work on that end." She took a deep breath. "But I'm betting all our hard work will pay off."

He slipped his arm around her waist. "I think so, too."

Then the lights went out and they were plunged into darkness. Megs sighed. "Oh, this can't be good."

ADAM COULD THINK of few things that were worse than being stranded in a theater with a beautiful woman you had feelings for and her kind and compassionate sister. The fact that without power, they also had no heat only made things interesting. He pulled his coat on and buried his hands in his pockets. "Maybe we should head home."

Megan nodded. "I promised you a ride home. The rest of this stuff can wait until tomorrow."

They gathered their belongings, Megan walking through one last time to make sure everything had been put away. Finally, she joined them at the side door, and Adam pushed it open.

Or tried to. He had to put his shoulder against it and then force his whole body against it before it opened. The three of them stared out into the world of white. The snow came down heavy, obscuring their view of anything beyond a foot in front of them. Adam slammed the door shut so that no more heat would escape.

Kelly turned to him. "What are you doing? We need to go home. We can't drive in this."

"I've driven through worse."

"It's not safe, Megan," he insisted, chastising himself for not realizing as soon as they'd stepped out of the theatre.

Kelly put a hand on her sister's arm. "He's right. We need to sit this out for a while." She rubbed her arms. "Let's see if we can find some old costumes or something to layer up and keep us warm."

Back inside the theatre, they found boxes of old clothes in a sort of dressing room.

Kelly put on an emerald green gown that looked queenly while Megan found several coats and handed them to Adam. She dug through the box more and found a cape and put that around herself. They settled into the green room that had a couch and was more enclosed so that it felt warmer. Kelly checked her cell phone. "No signal."

Adam and Megan checked theirs, but neither of theirs had a signal, either. Megan said, "Well, on the bright side, we're indoors and can stay relatively warm. And if we get hungry, I brought dessert."

Adam explored the green room and found a few older magazines. "And we've got reading material to keep us entertained."

Kelly cocked her head to the side. "Do you hear that?"

They all paused, and Adam could hear a pounding sound. He stood and motioned the women back. "I'll go check it out."

Megan shot to her feet. "We're going with you. Safety in numbers. We don't know who's trying to get in here."

Adam at least got to lead the way, and wrenched open the door. A figure completely covered in snow stood there. Kelly pushed past Adam. “Sam? What are you doing here?”

He stepped inside and pushed the hood off his head, releasing the layer of snow that covered him. Kelly embraced him. Sam kissed her forehead, cheeks, mouth. “I couldn’t get hold of you, so I got worried.”

“You’re crazy for going out in this.”

“I’m crazy about you.”

She let go of him long enough for him to remove his coat, then returned to his arms. Sam put his hands on either side of her face. “This isn’t the way I meant to do this, but when I couldn’t find you, I realized I don’t want to spend one single day without you again. Please, would you marry me?”

Megan grabbed Adam’s arm as Kelly stared at Sam, her eyes wide and her mouth hanging open. Then she started to nod, slowly at first then with more conviction. “Yes, of course. Yes!”

They kissed, and Megan led Adam back to the green room. “Let’s give them a moment.”

He took a seat on the couch and glanced over at her. “You approve of this guy?”

"More than approve." She grabbed one of the magazines. "He's one of the best men that I know. And they're perfect for each other." She flipped through a few pages. "Besides, he already asked for my blessing."

"And that's how you would want it done?"

She frowned at him, and he wasn't sure why her answer should matter. They were friends at her insistence that they couldn't be more. She shrugged. "I guess it depends on the guy and the situation."

The two lovebirds entered the green room, holding hands, their faces flushed with joy and passion. Megan rose to her feet and walked over to embrace the couple. "Congratulations. This is the best news."

Kelly showed off her hand, where a simple diamond ring now graced. "It's perfect, isn't it? And Sam said you already knew he was going to ask."

Sam sat on the couch and pulled Kelly down next to him. "Are you really upset by that?"

She shook her head and leaned into him. "No. But she could have at least given me a hint that this was coming."

"Give me a break." Megan smiled widely. "You had an idea it was coming, so don't even put this on me." She looked around the room. "I'm going to go get a pastry box in case we get hungry."

Adam stood, not wanting to be left alone with the loving couple. "I'll go with you."

They picked their way carefully through the darkened theater, Megan leading the way with the light from her cell phone while Adam held her hand so they wouldn't get separated. She pushed open the door that took them from the auditorium to the lobby. "I think I stored the boxes on the left."

"I thought they were on the right."

"Should we split up and both look?"

Adam squeezed her hand, not willing to let go of it so soon. "Let's stick together."

They walked to the left of the lobby, Megan putting the hand holding her cell phone out in front of her. She bumped into a table. "Found them."

She chose a box and turned, running into Adam's chest. He put a hand on her to steady her, then moved toward the doors that led to the auditorium. “I’ll take point on our journey back. But we should probably take our time. Give the engaged couple a few minutes alone.”

Megan slowed her steps. “I hope this blizzard blows over for us to have the fundraiser.”

“Worse comes to worst, we’ll delay it to Saturday to give everyone time to dig out.” Adam pulled her into a row of seats. “We’ve done all we can to make it successful.”

He rested his arm along the back of her seat, wanting to touch her but afraid of making her skittish. She put her head in the crook of his arm and sighed. It was the only encouragement he needed. He put his arms around her and pulled her tighter against him. She sighed again. “What are we doing?”

“Giving Sam and your sister some alone time.”

“I meant us. What are we doing about us?” She pulled away, and he regretted her absence. “I’m not sure how I feel about you.”

“Yes, you are, but you don’t want to deal

with it. That's why you keep getting close then pulling away, like you just did. You don't want to admit that there's more than friendship between us."

"We made a good team on the fund-raiser."

"It's more than that." He reached out and found her hand, stood and pulled her to her feet. "I think we should get back to the green room with dinner."

"You're angry."

"Not angry. Disappointed. I thought we might have had something between us."

"But..."

"It's a big risk, I get that. Especially with someone like me."

She followed behind him; he still had her hand in his, but he could feel her pulling away even as they approached the green room. Clearly, she didn't want to let herself get too close to him.

And he wasn't going to pursue someone who couldn't love him back.

He paused. Love? As she passed him and walked into the green room, he admitted that was what had happened. At least for him. He loved every part of her, including the part that would let him leave without her.

MEGS SHIFTED IN her chair and pressed the button on top of her phone. It was only a little past nine, but without lights it felt much later. Kelly yawned and stretched out next to Sam on the small two-seater sofa.

She peered in the dark at Adam's form propped against the wall by the door. He hadn't said much to her since they'd returned with the pastries. He had thanked her for thinking to bring them tonight rather than in the morning, since that meant they wouldn't starve, but she hadn't gotten any more out of him than that.

The problem was that he wanted more from her than she could give. No, more than she would give.

She'd lived twelve years with terrible guilt, transforming her life into one where she always made the safe choice. She followed the rules and did what was expected because that way no one was hurt.

Adam got to his feet. "I'll be back. I'm going to check the doors to make sure everything is secured."

"I'll go with you."

"No. I'm also going to find the restroom."

She sat back on the chair and pulled the crocheted afghan they'd found around her shoulders. She heard Adam leave the room. Sam whispered, "You okay, kid?"

"Why wouldn't I be?"

"Did something happen between you two?"

"No. Nothing can." She raised her arms above her head, released a deep breath and then lowered them.

"Do you want some advice?"

"About Adam? No."

Sam chuckled softly. "I'm giving it to you anyway." He paused, and Megs wasn't sure if he'd drifted off. Then his voice came through the darkness. "If Kelly had based her love for me on my past, we wouldn't be getting married. She'd probably run for the hills because of my drug addiction. But I'm thankful for every day she saw that I was a changed man and gave me a chance."

"It's not because of our past."

"Really? Because it seems as though you're still holding on to it pretty tightly.

Maybe it's to keep your friend alive at least in your memories."

"Kenny's never coming back."

"Exactly. And you could miss out on something amazing in your life because you'd rather snuggle up to a memory than a man who's alive and loves you."

Loves her? She couldn't wrap her mind around the idea. "He doesn't love me."

"I've seen how he looks at you. As if you're the best part of his day just by walking in the room. And if that isn't love, then I don't know what is."

Sam was wrong. Had to be. Because Adam couldn't love her. Grateful for the dark, she let the tears fall.

She pulled the afghan tighter around her, turning it into a cocoon that kept everyone out and herself safe inside.

THE LIGHTS TURNED back on at a little after three in the morning. Megs sat up in the chair and squinted at the brightness. Sam and Kelly still slept on the couch while Adam blinked at her from the opposite wall. She rose slowly, wiped her eyes and nudged Sam. "Hey, the power's back on."

He yawned and stretched while Kelly still clung to him. "We should check to see how bad it is out there. They might have the snow plows out already."

Adam stood and waved at them to stay where they were. "I'll go check."

"I'll follow you." Megs draped the blanket around Kelly. "I need to find the restroom anyway."

They walked silently backstage to the side door. Adam unbolted it and opened it, pushing about a pile of snow with the bottom of the metal door. He whistled. "All that white looks pretty."

The road didn't appear as if the plows had reached this far yet, however. Which meant they'd be stuck there for a while longer. Megs let him close the door while she walked to the lobby to find the restroom. Once she was finished, she splashed water on her face then used a paper towel to dry it off. Her eyes looked as if she'd fallen asleep crying. Which wasn't far from the truth. She'd covered her mouth to cover up her cries, hoping no one heard her.

Having stalled long enough, she walked into the lobby and found Adam waiting for her. His eyes lit up as she walked toward him, and she hated that it made her feel good. He held his hand out to her. She accepted it and walked with him back to the green room. "It could be hours before they dig us out."

"Probably."

She let go of his hand and pulled out her phone, checking to see if she had any bars. Yes. "The phones are working again."

"Do you need to call someone?"

She shook her head. The only people who would worry about her were here. "I wonder if we should let someone know we're stuck here. Maybe call the sheriff's office."

"They'll see our cars and figure it out."

"I guess you're right." She put her phone back into her pocket and stepped into the green room. Kelly still lay on the sofa, holding hands with Sam.

Megs looked away from the display of love and affection. She was happy for her sister. Truly, she was. But she ached to have it for herself. She glanced at Adam. He seemed to have some feelings for her. Even Sam said he could see it.

Maybe all she needed to do was accept what was held out to her. If she could trust it.

ADAM WATCHED THE sleeping couple for a while, then turned on his heel and left the green room. Like Megan, he couldn't fall back asleep. Too much energy or too many thoughts running around in the hamster wheel of his brain. He needed to do something, so he searched the backstage area for a janitor's closet and found one. Bryan had stored a snow shovel and a bucket of sidewalk salt there, so he grabbed both and took them with him to the lobby. He returned to the green room and quietly grabbed his jacket.

But not quiet enough since Megan stirred from her corner. "Where are you going?"

"I'm going to start digging us out."

She stood and grabbed her coat. "I'll help."

"No, you won't."

She stuffed her arms into the sleeves and zipped up her coat. Pulled hat and mittens on, then brushed past him and into the hallway. He followed after her. "The snow is heavy. You'll injure yourself trying to shovel it."

She stopped walking up the aisle of the auditorium and stalked back to him. "And what about you? You bumped your head pretty good yesterday. Should you be out there in this weather?"

"Are you always this stubborn?"

"It's called persistence. And it's the right thing to do." She turned back and finished the walk through the auditorium to the lobby.

Adam paused long enough to put on his coat and gloves before taking the shovel from her. He pointed to the bucket. "I'll do the heavy work. You can put the ice melt on after I'm finished."

She shook her head. "Who's the stubborn one now?"

The front doors opened easily since the entrance was a courtyard covered by a tall roof that had rows of light bulbs lining it. Megan had turned them on to give them enough light to do what they needed to do.

Despite the covering, wind had caused snowdrifts to gather against the doors and windows and in the corners, so he focused on clearing those first. Megan sprinkled the sidewalk salt on any icy patches. Once the courtyard had been cleared, they stepped out closer to the curb and surveyed the parking lot. Adam grimaced. He couldn't use the shovel to clear the lot, but he could concentrate on the sidewalks. He put his head down and began to shovel.

Once his fingers froze to the point of becoming useless, he walked back to the lobby to warm up a little. The grand clock at the entrance to the auditorium read that it was almost five in the morning. He pulled his cell phone from his jeans pocket and dialed Dave's phone number. His district manager was the ultimate authority to close the branch due to weather, but Adam could advise him on the conditions in Lake Mildred. The call went to voice mail, and Adam informed his supervisor that he was currently stranded at the theater due to the road conditions and requested a call back to determine if the branch should open.

He put his phone away and stretched. Megan walked into the lobby and put the bucket down near the front doors. She slipped her gloves off, then blew on her fingers. “This is crazy. Why did we volunteer to do this?”

“I think Rick used guilt against us.” Adam opened a pastry box and pulled out a mini blueberry-lemon tart. He popped it into his mouth and chewed, appreciating how Megan had kept the sweet of the berry without losing the tang of the lemon. “You have a gift.”

She covered her yawn with her hand but waved him off. “I was taught by the best.” She glanced around the lobby and sighed. “All this work, and it could be for nothing.”

“Don’t talk like that. We can still make this happen.”

“We need an act of nature to not only clear all this snow from the parking lot, but to get everyone else dug out and the roads cleared.” She slumped against one of the tables, and a prize clipboard jostled onto the floor. She bent over to pick it up. “As you can tell, I’m not exactly cheerful and optimistic in the morning.”

“It’s not even five. I don’t expect anything.” He massaged the back of his neck where a crick had formed. “I wonder if Bryan has a coffee machine in his office.”

"I can do even better. I had the big coffee urns from my bakery transported here for the fund-raiser along with supplies. Give me ten minutes, and I'll have your caffeine fix ready." She rose to her feet and glanced around the lobby. "All I need to do is figure out which boxes they're in."

With his help, Megan found what she was looking for, and soon the aroma of coffee perking tingled his nose. He sniffed appreciatively. Ambrosia.

Sam stumbled into the lobby, squinting at the lights they'd turned on. "Do I smell coffee?"

The men gathered near the theater bar and sighed as Megan poured them each a cup of fragrant brew. Sam took his cup to the front doors and peered out into the snow. "It's going to take us all day to get this place cleared."

Adam joined him and nodded. "Megan and I got most of the sidewalks, but we didn't even attempt to tackle the lot."

A truck with a plow attached to the front of it pulled into the lot. Adam pointed it out to them. "Or maybe we'll have an angel arrive with a snow plow."

Megan rushed to the windows and smiled. "An angel who happens to own the theater." She watched for a few moments. "For a Texas boy, he sure knows how to clear the snow."

Adam glanced at Sam, who gave a short nod. They put on their coats, hats and gloves, then went to join Bryan. There was no way Adam was going to let two men from the South show up one born in the frozen north.

MEGS BREWED MORE coffee as the men cleared both the front and side parking lots where the talent show acts would be arriving. She used a serving tray to set out pastries and found the napkins she'd packed to be used later. It wasn't much, but they'd probably appreciate a hot drink and a sweet treat after battling the elements.

The sun had started to rise by the time they entered the lobby, stomping their boots and removing their gloves that had gotten wet. She took their outerwear and hung it up in the coatroom off the lobby and returned to find them joking about the weather while they ate her pastries. Bryan bit into a bear claw, and his eyebrows raised. “My, my, Miss Sweet, you do know your way around a doughnut.”

“I should.” She refreshed their coffees and set out more sugar and creamer packets. “I’ll probably need to go back to the Sweetheart to pick up more supplies before the fund-raiser tonight.”

The three men looked at each other and avoided her eyes. “What?”

Adam cleared his throat and put his cheese croissant back on his plate. “Bryan said that the sheriff closed the roads until further notice. Plows are out, but it’s going to be at least tomorrow before they can get everyone moving again.”

“Oh.” She’d been hoping that Bryan’s appearance meant things weren’t as bad as she feared. “I’ll have to make some calls to let everyone know that we’re postponing the talent show until tomorrow night.”

Adam put a hand on her shoulder. “We might want to wait until next weekend. They’re predicting another storm to come through tonight.”

She put down her coffee. “No. The kids in the show are depending on this.” And so was she. She'd put all her hopes into this one evening. If they could pull this off, then there wasn't anything they couldn't do. "One night won't make a difference, but a week could mean acts will drop out."

"Then, we'll hope the weather forecaster is wrong."

Bryan took another pastry from the tray. "I'll help any way I can if you keep feeding me like this." He licked his fingers. "Man, when is your bakery reopening? I gotta get me some of this."

"Two weeks. I hope."

Sam nodded. "We can make it work."

Kelly drifted into the lobby. "Did I miss the party?"

Megs poured her some coffee and handed it to her sister with two packets of sugar and one of cream. "The roads are still closed, so we're making do here."

Kelly doctored her coffee, then cradled the cup in her hands. "We're going to have to let the grapevine know that the show's been postponed to tomorrow."

Adam held up his hand. "I'm on it." He opened his cell phone and dialed a number. When the person on the other end answered, he said, "Eva, glad I got hold of you. Dave's going to keep our branch closed until noon today to give us all time to dig out. Can you let the other employees know?" He nodded at whatever she said, then he glanced at Megs. "Also, can you get the word out that we're going to delay the fund-raiser one night? That would be great."

When he hung up, he shrugged. "Done. I swear that woman knows everyone in this town and the next one over."

"So now that we have that covered, how are we going to get out of here?" Megs walked to the windows and looked out into the world of white. She turned back. "Not that I haven't enjoyed being stranded with you, but it's time to go."

Kelly wrapped one arm around Sam's waist. "I don't know. Being snowed in together wasn't so bad, was it?"

Megs glanced at Adam, who was watching her. She looked away and started to clean up their mess from breakfast. It hadn't been bad. Not at all.

In fact, she felt closer to Adam than she ever had. As if more barriers between them had fallen away. She wondered what that meant for their future, if they even had a chance for one.

CHAPTER EIGHT

AFTER ALL THEIR hard work, the evening of the fund-raiser had arrived, even if it was a day later than originally planned. Megs brushed the skirt of her gold silk gown to smooth it out. She counted the trays of pastries and the urns of coffee. Check. She walked by the tables where the prize clipboards waited to be auctioned. Check. The ushers she'd hired to hand out programs waited in white shirts and black bowties at the entrances to the auditorium. Check.

Acts for the talent show had been arriving since four o'clock to rehearse. She could hear a dance routine performing onstage while a soloist warmed up, singing scales. Ticket sellers waited in the booth to sell last-minute seats for those who hadn't purchased them in advance. If they sold only twenty more seats, they'd have two hundred in the audience for the evening.

Adam walked down the curving staircase from the balcony and joined her near the theater bar. He whistled at her, and she blushed as she pushed her bangs back from her warm face. "You look as though you've been dipped in gold."

She should have whistled back at him. Adam in a suit looked good, but in a tuxedo he was mouthwatering. "You look good, too."

He smiled and tugged on the lapel of his jacket. "This old thing?" He laughed and let his gaze move around the room. "It looks as if we're ready."

"We'll open the doors an hour before the show." She consulted the grand clock above the theater doors. "In about five minutes."

"I'll let everyone know to get to their stations."

Before he could leave, she grabbed his arm. "Do you think the audience will show? Even with the roads?"

He brushed her bangs to the side. "They won't be able to stay away."

She pressed a hand to her belly and nodded. "Right." She turned back to make sure all the serving trays were full and ready to go. She'd hired her baker and cashier for the evening to keep everything stocked and moving. It felt good to be back with her team even for one evening. In two weeks, it would be more permanent. And she was ready.

In a pink gown, Kelly walked up to her. She held the microphone that she would use as co-emcee. "Sam is having a meltdown backstage."

"Stage fright?"

"One of his guitar springs broke." Kelly waved off Megs's exclamations. "He's got extras, but his nerves are getting to him more than usual. It'll be fine."

"Is my song ready?"

Kelly nodded. "Are you ready to hear it?"

"I need to. It's not only for Kenny, but anyone out there like him going through some major stuff." She put a hand on Kelly's arm. "Thank you for doing this."

"Always." She glided away.

"Quite an opening for my old lady." Bryan, too, wore a tuxedo but had opted for a string tie. "You're making her look good tonight."

"You did all the hard work."

"I had help. But then I don't think there's anything that man wouldn't do for you."

Megs frowned. He had to be mistaken. "You mean anything for the fund-raiser."

"Honey, you could ask for the moon and that man would build a rocket to fetch it for you." He tipped an imaginary cowboy hat, then walked past her to the front doors and opened them with a flourish. "Ladies and gentlemen, the Starlit Theater is now open for business."

The next hour was spent checking to make sure that people found their seats. That the silent-auction items received bids. That VIPs sat in the boxes around the stage. That talent acts waited backstage and knew their order of appearance. She flitted from one part of the theater to another as needed and paused only a minute to take off one high heel and massage her aching foot.

At seven o'clock, the lights flickered, then dimmed. Onstage, Sam and Kelly welcomed the audience to the talent show and introduced the first act, Kelly's friend from high school, Penny Sorenson. She sounded amazing, her voice tinged with a hint of sorrow as she sang about living separate lives. She closed her eyes as she finished the song and tilted her head back, but opened them as the audience applauded.

"It's a great turnout."

She turned and nodded at Adam. "Better than I'd hoped." She watched as Penny took a bow onstage and the curtains fell. She glanced at the program and waved on the barbershop quartet that included the city inspector, Will Stone, and her accountant, Jack Novakowski. "Break a leg."

The curtains went up, and they started with a few jokes about the snowstorm before singing about summertime.

Megs reached over and took Adam's hand. "I don't have the final figures yet, but the numbers look great." She smiled up at him. "You did a good thing for the community."

"We did." He squeezed her hand, then pulled her farther into the wings, away from the stage. "Listen, I know that it's been weird between us, but I…"

The barbershop quartet ended to loud applause. Megs let go of Adam and consulted the program. The four-year-old dance class was next, but she didn't see them preparing to take the stage. She held up her finger to Adam. "Hold on to that thought. We're missing the Pixie Sticks." She searched behind the curtains until she found Mrs. Jensen preparing the future ballerinas for their dance. Relieved, she returned to Adam, crisis averted.

He pulled her back to the green room, which was empty and shut the door. "I need to do this before I lose my nerve." Then he pushed her against the wall and kissed her.

His mouth was warm and tasted like one of her cinnamon twists. She grabbed his shoulders to keep from sliding to the floor in a puddle. She kissed him back, unwilling to think beyond that moment. Letting that kiss be everything in that second. Not letting thoughts take her to where she didn't want to go. Keeping the past where it belonged.

He whispered her name against her mouth. "I can't stop thinking about you. And believe me, I've tried."

Megs shushed him and pulled him into another kiss, reveling in the way it made her feel to be in his arms.

He broke off the kiss. "We need to talk. Maybe after the show?"

She nodded and gave him another peck before checking her hair in the mirror and walking out of the green room, pretending as if nothing had happened when actually the bottom had dropped out of her world.

ADAM WATCHED AS Megan ushered the acts onstage before they were announced. She and her sister had done a wonderful job finding a variety of singers, dancers, magicians and comedians. Including the current one, Rick Allyn the mayor, doing stand-up. Granted, he did it badly but the audience enjoyed his effort. Adam applauded at the end of his five-minute act.

He consulted his own program. Only one act remained, Sam and Kelly singing a new, original song. He'd been there the night they'd premiered "The Hole Inside." The aching honesty of their performance had brought tears to many there, and had even made Adam choke up a little. He looked forward to hearing another one.

Rick walked offstage and pounded Adam

on the back. “This has been an amazing night. Thank you.”

“For giving you a stage and an audience?”

Rick shook his head. “For showing up and being there for the community when they needed you.”

Adam shrugged and turned his attention as the curtains opened, and Sam walked out with his guitar and motioned to the other side of the stage where Kelly entered. They met in the middle, then looked out at the audience. Kelly adjusted the microphones and smiled. “Tonight, I’m proud to premiere another original song. This one has a deep personal meaning to someone close to us who asked us to write it for her. We call it ‘Wish I’d Told You.’”

Sam strummed on his guitar, then Kelly started to sing. “Don’t give up, just hold on. This monster can’t hold you for long. You’re stronger and better than him. Don’t give in to his words, he’s wrong.”

Together they sang about things they wish they would have said. How they’d fight off the dragons until the person was strong enough to do it on their own. Kelly closed her eyes as she sang, "But now you're gone, and I'm still here. The things I wish I said."

He looked across the stage where Megan stood in the wings on the other side. She watched Sam and Kelly as they continued the song, tears streaming down her face. They'd written the song for her.

Sam took up the song then. "You're better, you're stronger. You can hold on much longer. Don't give in to the dark, let it take you away. You can be here to fight another day."

The song might as well have been called Kenny's Song because that was who it was about. It was what Megan thought and felt about what happened.

"I put on the guilt. I wore my own shame."

Yep. She'd said as much to him before. But the song spoke about monsters and dragons. Was that what she thought of him still? What? He was good enough for the odd kiss, but not for more?

He shook his head and turned to walk back to the green room. He couldn't take any more rejection.

"I should have told you, but now you're gone. And I have to move on. I move on."

APPLAUSE ERUPTED AFTER Sam and Kelly finished singing. They took a bow and walked offstage.

Jack had handed Megs the final figures, not including the silent auction, which would continue until the last person left. Megs looked around for Adam. They were supposed to announce together the money raised that evening, then crown the winner of the talent show. But instead, Sam thrust the microphone into her hand and pushed her onstage. She winced in the bright lights and used the note card that held the figures as a shield. She tried to smile, but all those eyes on her made her knees wobble and her stomach lurch.

Then Kelly stood next to her, putting her arm around her waist. "While the judges complete their scoring of tonight's acts, Megan Sweet has an announcement." She nudged her sister.

Megs glanced at the note card and held the microphone up to her mouth. "Thanks to your generosity and support tonight, we've already raised twelve thousand dollars. With the proceeds from the silent auction, we expect to pass the twenty-five-thousand-dollar mark. So thank you all. And don't forget there's still time to bid on some terrific prize packages in the lobby."

Again, she looked around, hoping to see Adam. He'd been on the other side of the stage while Sam and Kelly had sung her song. But then he'd disappeared. She shielded her eyes with the note card. "Is Adam Hawkins still here? He was an instrumental part of our success tonight."

He walked by the front of the stage, then took the steps on the side, carrying a folded piece of paper in his hand. He took the microphone from Megs without looking at her. "I'm pleased to announce that the judges have made their decision. In third place, we have the Pixie Sticks dance class."

The teachers herded the four-year-olds onto the stage, where they waved to the crowd amid the applause. Adam consulted the paper again. "In second place, we have Lake Mildred High's glee club." The kids raced to their place on the side of the stage and took a group bow. "And in first place…" Adam paused and cleared his throat. "Penny Sorenson."

Kelly gave a shriek and clapped even harder. When the other woman walked onto the stage, the two women embraced before Kelly handed her the microphone. "Thank you. I only wish my husband had been here to see this." She put her arm around Kelly's waist. "But I think it's only fair that we hear that new song again. What do you say?"

Kelly shook her head until the crowd started chanting her name and Sam's. Finally she nodded and held out her hand to Sam who joined her in the middle of the stage. As they started singing again, Adam pulled Megs into the right wing offstage and glared at her. "Is that really what you think of me? I'm a monster?"

She shook her head, but he'd already walked away and out into the audience. Megs pasted the smile on her face, but hearing the song again only made it hurt all the more. Especially when they sang the last part, "I should have told you, but now you're gone. And I have to move on. I move on."

She wiped away the tears, then clapped

her hands as she approached the middle of the stage where Sam and Kelly stood. She took the microphone. "Thank you all again for your generosity and your support. Drive safely and have a wonderful evening."

She followed in the direction that Adam had taken earlier. She congratulated Jack on his performance in the barbershop quartet as she passed him, but kept her eye out for Adam. She spotted him heading to the front of the theater accompanied by Bryan. She called his name and tried to walk faster, but her heels kept her from catching up with him. Instead, she saw the back of him walk out the front of the theater and disappear into the night.

She turned and found Bryan waiting for her. "He said he'd talk to you tomorrow when you're doing the cleanup. He wasn't ready to talk tonight."

"Did he seem angry?"

Bryan gave a shrug. "More as though he's got a bee in his bonnet that won't let him be." He glanced around as the crowds still milled in the lobby of the theater. "I've gotten a lot of compliments on the theater tonight. I even had the dance studio director ask about renting the space for their spring recital in a couple of months."

Megs smiled. "That's great news, Bryan. Congratulations."

"I guess it's a banner night for the both of us."

Then, why did she feel as though she'd lost something important?

MEGS ARRIVED AT the theater on Sunday morning at nine thirty, earlier than they'd agreed on, but she didn't want Adam to have the chance to sneak out before they had an opportunity to talk. Because they needed to clear the air.

And she needed to figure out how she felt about him.

The only car in the parking lot was Bryan's silver pickup truck. She parked next to it, then got out of her car and walked to the front doors. They were locked, so she knocked on them until Bryan appeared to let her in.

"I'm surprised you're here already. It was a late night last night."

She yawned as if to give his statement credit, then looked around the lobby. The tables had already been taken down and put away. Boxes contained the prize clipboards. She turned back to Bryan. “Looks as if everything is already done. Adam was here already?”

“He got here about eight this morning. Said he had something important to do today.” He pointed to the boxes. “He said you’d know what to do with the winners of the auction.”

She nodded. “I’ll load them in my car and make the phone calls this afternoon.”

“I’ll give you a hand with the boxes.”

Together, they loaded everything, as well as the coffee urns from her bakery into her car. Bryan tried to give back the pastries that hadn’t been eaten, but she waved off the suggestion. “Help yourself. I have more of them at home.”

With her car loaded and the theater emptied, she knew she should go home. But that held little appeal. So she drove to the Sweetheart. Might as well return the coffee urns and check on the progress of her bakery. She unlocked the back door, then propped it open so she could get the boxes inside. After her first trip, she snapped on the light and took a deep breath as she surveyed her kitchen. It was almost perfect. Perfect would be when she got the clearance from the town inspector to start working again.

With the coffee urns unloaded and washing in the new dishwasher, she walked into the front room. She snapped on a utility light attached to the scaffolding that took up most of the space. So much left to do in here, but Sam had promised two more weeks. Fourteen more days, and she could go back to her normal life. She could be the baker she knew to be.

A knock on the back door. She walked through the kitchen and found Shane standing there. "Congratulations on the fundraiser last night. Seemed as though you were able to raise a lot of money."

"Thank you again for the donation of the aquarium. It went for a lot more than I expected." She invited him in, wishing she had some kind of bread or pastry to give him. "But that's not why you stopped by, is it?"

"Adam's been on my case to come to him for a business loan. Seems to think that he can help me, but I'm not sure if I can trust him." Shane leaned on the marble island. "What made you change your mind?"

"Honestly? He was my last resort, but he proved to be a strong ally. He helped me get through the entire process and pushed to get what I needed." And she hadn't really thanked him enough for it. That added another layer to her guilt. But Shane wasn't here about that. "You should at least give him a call to see what he can do for you. What do you have to lose?"

"So you trust him now? Even after everything that happened?"

"In spite of the past, yes I do. Because he's a changed man."

Shane nodded. "All right, then." He glanced around the kitchen. "Looks as though you're really coming along."

"Two more weeks, I hope."

"They're reopening the hardware store tomorrow. It's good to see us bounce back."

He gave a sigh, and Megs put her hand on his arm. "You will, too. And you'll be better than before."

"Thanks, Megs. And for the advice."

"Call him."

Shane nodded and walked out the back door. Following her own advice, she took her cell phone from her jeans pocket and dialed Adam's number. The call went straight to voice mail. She waited for the beep before leaving a brief message. Then she texted him, I was at the theater, but you beat me to it. Thanks.

She waited, but there was no reply. Now she knew what it felt like to be the one wanting to make an effort, but being avoided. And she didn't like it one bit.

ADAM'S PHONE BUZZED, but he ignored it again. He knew he'd told Megan that they would talk today, but he couldn't. Not yet.

He pulled into the parking lot of the bank, though it was Sunday. He wanted to drop off the deposit they'd collected the previous evening and put it in the night-drop slot. With finishing at the theater so early, he had the rest of the day free and no plans.

His phone buzzed again. He rolled his eyes and checked the screen. Not a familiar phone number. "Adam Hawkins."

"Hey, it's Shane."

Adam paused. “Okay.”

“I’ve been thinking about what you said. And I really do need help.”

That was a huge change of heart. “What brought this about?”

“I talked to Megs about it this morning. And to be honest, the phone call I made the other day.”

The one to his dad. He could imagine how that conversation had gone. “Did my dad tell you to trust me?”

“No, quite the opposite, in fact. He called you worthless and no good.” The other man paused. “I remember the names he’d call you. The way he treated you, and me if I was over at your house. You didn’t have much of a chance to be anything than what you were taught to be back then. I haven’t really given you an opportunity for me to get to know the man you are now.”

“Do you have plans this morning? We could meet over breakfast.”

“I’d like that.”

They met at a restaurant in Robert Falls, since Rick’s diner was closed on Sundays. Adam got there first and put their name on the waiting list, then paced in the foyer until Shane got there. The other man didn't shake his hand and kept his distance. Not that Adam could blame him. After all, he'd stuffed him in his own locker often enough. Or stuck his head in the boys' toilet and flushed it. Or spray painted names on his garage.

He had a lot to make up for.

The hostess called his name, and the two men followed her to a table by the window. Adam read over the menu, though he already knew what he was going to order. Putting a barrier between them for a moment. Giving him some time to collect his thoughts.

After they ordered, Adam fiddled with the silverware. Shane smiled. "It's okay. I'm nervous about this, too."

"We used to be best friends. I spent more summer nights in a tent in your backyard than I did at any campground." Adam placed his napkin in his lap and smoothed it out. "Then in high school, I became a real jerk to you."

Shane nodded. "Yes, you were. The best day of my senior year was the day you got sent away. I didn't wake up with bellyaches or headaches after that. I actually looked forward to going to school. Mostly because you weren't there."

He deserved to hear this. To see how he'd affected Shane's life. "I apologize for how I treated you. You didn't deserve it."

"No, I didn't."

Silence fell as the waitress brought their breakfasts and refilled their coffee cups. After she left, Adam held out his business card. "If you're serious about getting a loan for your business, I really want to help you out."

"Megs said you went to bat for her."

"I did." Adam concentrated on pouring maple syrup over his French toast. "What else did she say?"

"That you've really changed."

Adam looked up. "She said that?" Shane nodded, and it gave Adam a sliver of hope. But first things first. "So what are you looking for in a loan? Terms, interest rates? What do you want to accomplish?"

For the next hour, they hammered out details for the business loan, and Shane left with the promise to come in with the paperwork that Adam would need to submit with the application. As they walked to their cars, Shane turned and gave a wave. "Call her, would you?"

He didn't need to say her name for Adam to know who he meant.

Adam got into his truck and started the drive back to Lake Mildred. His cell phone buzzed, but an unknown phone number popped up on the screen. He paused for a minute then answered it. "Hello?"

"Mr. Hawkins, it's Keegan. From a few weeks ago?"

"I remember." He waited to see if the kid would offer any more. But he stayed silent on the other end. "Did you need to talk?" He listened to the kid breathe on the other end of the call, but waited. "You called me."

"I can't make it stop."

"It's not easy, but you can."

"How? It's as if the anger boils up inside until I have to lash out, and I can't control it." It sounded as though the kid was crying on the other end, but Adam didn't want to risk ending the conversation too soon, so he let the kid talk. "It's as if the words have to come out. And I hate him even more for taking it without flinching, and I hate myself even more for saying them."

"Him?"

"Derek in my math class."

"Words are very powerful."

"Tell me about it."

"But, Keegan, you're bigger than those words." Adam rubbed the bridge of his nose. "One thing military school taught me is that I could control what I say and what I do. Those impulses you get don't have to rule you. It's the other way around if you're willing to work at it."

"How?"

"By learning new ways to cope with what's going on at home or at school." Adam racked his brain for what had worked for him. "I took up boxing, which sounds like the opposite of what you want, but I learned how to control my emotions and my body. There's nothing like hitting a punching bag until all that anger is spent." More silence. "Talking about it helps, too. Like what you did today, calling me because you don't want to keep doing this. It's a big first step."

"I guess."

"So what happened today?"

They spent the next half hour talking about Keegan's anger and his relationship with his mom. Adam could draw so many parallels between this kid and himself. They ended the call with Keegan promising to check in with Adam later in the week. "And I've got a visitor pass for my gym if you want to try that punching bag."

"Yeah, maybe."

MEGS HAD ALREADY called four of the winners of the silent auction. She liked making these kinds of calls where the person on the other end was so excited. She checked off the name of her last call and picked up the next clipboard. It was a romantic dinner for two at The Vineyard. She moved her finger down the list and paused at the name. Adam Hawkins for three thousand dollars. He'd outbid everyone else by more than triple. She didn't have to glance at the phone number to reach him. She knew it by heart by now.

The phone rang three times, then went to voice mail. She paused, then rushed out with "Congratulations, Adam. You won the romantic dinner for two at The Vineyard with a bid for three thousand dollars. Please call me back on this number so that we can make arrangements for payment and delivery. Thank you."

She hung up the phone, then took a deep breath. Picked up the next clipboard and started to dial that winner's phone number when a knock sounded at the front door. She clicked off her phone, then got up from the dining room table and walked through the living room. Checked the window to see who was there. She opened the front door before she lost her nerve. "Hi, Adam."

"Hey."

Silence, and neither one moved. She didn't invite him in but he didn't ask to come in, either. One of them should say something, do something, but she didn't know who should start. Finally, she said, "I don't think you're a monster. Not anymore."

"But you did before?"

She'd called him worse names after she found out Kenny had died. "Yes."

"When you applied for the loan last month, did you still think I was?"

"I didn't know what to think. I didn't

know you anymore. Only who you used to be." She had tried so hard to reconcile the man before her then with the boy who had tormented her best friend. Even if she squinted, it was hard to see that angry bully. "But now I'm sure you're not."

Adam leaned against the door frame. "Then, why did you ask your sister to write that song?"

"Those were my feelings twelve years ago. You keep saying that I can't hold your past against you. That doesn't mean it's okay to hold it against me, either."

"I don't know what to do with you, Megan. Part of me wants to hold you in my arms. The other wants to run in the other direction because I can't handle being rejected again."

"Which part is stronger?"

He ran a hand through his hair. "I don't know. Maybe we can't let go of the past."

She nodded and tried not to let the tears already clogging her throat fall from her eyes. "I see."

He handed her a check. "For my dinner."

Megs walked back to the dining room table and pulled the gift certificate from the prize box. She returned and handed it to him. "I hope you enjoy it."

"Thank you." He tapped it against his leg a few times. "Well, I should go. Goodbye, Megan."

She nodded. "Goodbye." And it felt as though it was for good.

CHAPTER NINE

MEGS PUT THE hard hat on and stepped slowly into her bakery. Sam turned at her approach. "The city inspector should be here any minute to give us the clearance to go ahead and reopen."

She couldn't squelch the smile. "Good. And three days ahead of schedule, which will give me plenty of time to get everything organized. I can probably head to my supplier after the inspection and pick up the first round of supplies I'll need."

Sam cocked an eyebrow. "Let's wait on that until the city inspector signs off on it. Just in case."

"He will. He has to. You do great work."

"Doesn't mean he'll find something I've missed."

She doubted it, but she let him be cautious for now. At ten o'clock on the dot, someone knocked on the front door of the

Sweetheart. Megs ran to answer it and opened the door for Will Stone, the town inspector. He nodded approvingly at their hard hats. "I'm glad that you're taking the safety of this so seriously. And it's a good indication of what I'll find."

He brought out his tablet and booted up the program. He worked his way methodically around the front room, inspecting electrical sockets as well as the structure of the walls. He used a stylus to make notes on his tablet, then moved to the next section. He pulled out a small flashlight and checked the cupboards under the register as well as the glass display cases. More notes.

Megs longed to follow him around, hoping to catch a glimpse of what he was writing, but she stayed where she was. She needed the inspection to go well. Had to reopen the bakery because she needed something to go right in her life. Adam still avoided her after almost two weeks, and she missed him.

Sam nudged her from her daydreaming as Will moved to the kitchen. The biggest problems could be in this room, so she held her breath and watched him. He checked the appliances, the water pressure in the dish sink, and started up the dishwasher. He opened the walk-in refrigerator and strode inside, coming out after a few seconds and making more notes. He looked up at her once, then quickly moved on to the next item on his checklist.

When he walked outside to start the exterior inspection, Megs collapsed on a stool. "This is going to kill me."

"It might give you an ulcer, but you won't die." Sam leaned against the marble counter and crossed his arms over his chest. "I stand by my work, but he might have some things we need to tweak."

"Tweak?" She groaned and covered her face with her hands.

Will returned to the kitchen and placed his tablet on the counter. He looked the two of them over. "Well, which do you want first? The good news or the bad news?"

Sam looked at Megs. She shrugged. "Bad news first."

"There's three things that need to be fixed before you open." He started counting them off on his fingers. "The temperature of the hot-water heater is about two degrees below what it should be, so you'll want to adjust that. The electrical outlet in the restroom needs to be changed to a GFCI receptacle."

Megs frowned. "That's only two."

"The third is I want to order a special dessert for Suzy. She's been craving your cinnamon rolls lately, and no substitute will work." He pulled out his wallet. "I'm willing to pay in advance if you can make them for her."

Megs held out her hand. "You've got a deal."

Will smiled and shook her hand. "I'm getting the better end of it, but a lot of people will be glad when you reopen."

"I hope so."

He shook Sam's hand. "I'll email you the paperwork when I get back into the office. I can set up the re-inspection for tomorrow morning same time?"

"How about four this afternoon? I can get those items completed in the next hour."

Will shook Sam's hand. "Four o'clock." He glanced at Megs with a hopeful expression on his face.

She laughed. "Yes, I'll have the cinnamon rolls ready, too. I'll have to go home and make the dough now so they have plenty of time to rise." She looked around. "Unless you two need me any longer."

She left the bakery feeling as if things were headed in the right direction. But as she passed the bank on her way home, she tried not to let Adam's absence sour her day.

ADAM HANDED THE next page to Shane for his signature. He pointed to several places. "This is the interest rate on the loan. The length of the loan as well as the monthly payment." He turned the page over. "This amortization chart indicates how much interest you'll pay over the life of the loan."

Shane nodded and signed the page. He handed the sheet to Adam. "I really appreciate how quickly you were able to pull this off. You kept your word."

"I told you I would." He shuffled the papers and straightened them into a neat pile before placing them in a folder and handing it to Shane. "The check from the loan is in the front, and all you need to do is sign the back and deposit it into the account that we set up for you last week. You'll be able to draw on it right away for any repairs."

Shane held out the check and whistled. "Never thought I'd see the day I'd have money like this in my account." He stood and shook Adam's hand. "Thank you again."

"Took you long enough to trust me."

"No one said I was easy." He folded his coat over his arm. "Did you call Megs yet?"

Adam offered him a few business cards. "If you know anyone else who's looking for help, give them my card, okay?"

"And you said I was stubborn."

"My relationship with Megan is complicated." He opened the office door and let Shane pass. "What would you think about putting an aquarium in the lobby here?"

Shane nodded. "We can discuss it once I reopen."

"Sounds like a plan." Adam watched Shane walk up to the teller line to deposit his check. It made him feel good to know that he'd helped another person get closer to their goals. Especially someone who had resisted him so long in the beginning.

Eva's voice came over the intercom. "Mr. Thompson on line two for you, Adam."

Adam walked back behind his desk and picked up the phone. "Dave, this is a surprise."

"Let me tell you what's a surprise. In the past two weeks, I've gotten calls from about twenty citizens of Lake Mildred praising the work you've been doing at the branch." Dave paused. "They said they're bringing their accounts to the bank if they haven't already. And they'll recommend us to their family and friends."

"Really?" Adam rubbed his top lip, trying not to smile at this. "That is good to hear."

"Eva said that business is picking up on the teller line, too. And she attributes that to you and your leadership in the community."

"Thanks, Dave. You know I've always tried to do my best."

"And your best might have gotten you a promotion. How do you feel about managing more than one branch? I've got two branches in the Upper Peninsula that need a strong manager. You'd be perfect for the job. It would come with a substantial raise, as well. What do you say?"

That sounded awful nice. It had been what he'd been working toward professionally all these years after all. To get promoted and move up within the bank. To establish himself as a positive player within the community, too.

But coming back to Lake Mildred and proving himself to the town had been important. And he wasn't sure if he could turn his back on them right now. They had come a long way, but there was still progress to be made. Minds to be changed and hearts to be won. That personal goal of his was all important.

"Dave, it sounds good, but I need to think about it. Perhaps over the weekend?"

"Okay, but don't take too long to make up your mind. Those branches need a manager yesterday, and I can't sit on this."

Adam promised to give him an answer by Monday and hung up the phone. It was a good job offer that would challenge him and give him room to grow. So why wasn't he more excited about it?

Because the prospect of leaving Lake Mildred and Megan Sweet made the offer hollow. He swallowed at the bitterness that had gathered at the back of his throat and rose to his feet. He needed to fax Shane's paperwork over to the loan department.

BY FRIDAY EVENING, the town inspector had signed off on the improvements to the bakery, so Megs drove to her supplier in Robert Falls the next morning. She had a list of supplies she would need to get her through the first few days of being open before her regular order started being delivered. She loaded the back of Sam's pickup truck that she'd borrowed so she could get everything to the bakery in one trip. She loaded it down with fifty-pound bags of various flours, several forty-pound bags of sugar and large containers of spices.

She then drove to the home-goods store and browsed the kitchen department. She'd replaced most of her damaged equipment, but she wanted to pick something new up that would represent the new bakery. She perused the baking sheets and pans. Examined the rows of whisks and wooden spoons. Too practical.

She poked through the kitchen linens section. She had bought utilitarian towels and oven mitts, but she was drawn to the wall of brightly colored pot holders and dishcloths. She picked up a set of kitchen towels in a neon orange. The color made her happy, and she put them in the hand basket under her arm.

She walked to the line of registers, but paused when she saw a small sign that read, "Second chances are not given to make things right, but are given to prove that we could be even better if we fall." She picked it up. It summarized what had been her life the past six months since Grammy had died. She'd been given the chance to make things right with her sister, with Adam and in her life. She'd had to fall on her face and lose it all to see that she could make things better. She could be better.

She picked up the plaque and put it in her basket. She knew the perfect spot to hang it in the kitchen at the bakery.

After she paid for her purchases, she drove back to Lake Mildred and to the Sweetheart. She unloaded Sam's truck, then searched for the tool kit Sam had given her to fix things that might come up. Inside the kit, she found a hammer and nail. Underneath the silver clock, she hung the sign. It would be a reminder of how far she'd come and how much further she could go.

With everything put away, she walked through the bakery one last time. Ingredients were stocked. Equipment waited to be used. The new taller tables and chairs for the front room were ready to be occupied. The cash register wanted to ring up purchases and fill with money. She smiled. She was almost ready.

When she thought about the reopening, she wanted three people to be there. One, her sister, would be. The second, her grandmother, would only be there in spirit. But the last, Adam, would only be there if she swallowed her pride and asked him.

These past couple of weeks without him had shined a light on how empty her life truly was. True, she had her sister and Sam. But when she saw the two of them, she longed to find love in her life, too. She thought she might have found it with Adam, but they had too much in their past to get beyond it.

Loving Adam meant letting go of Kenny. And she'd held on to his memory so long that she didn't know what would happen if she released him once and for all. To liberate herself from the guilt and shame. To truly let him stay buried and in peace.

It was a chance she would have to take. She pulled out her cell phone and checked for Adam's name before sending the call. It rang three times then went to voice mail. She took a deep breath. "Hey, Adam. It's Megs. I got the clearance to reopen the bakery, so I'm having a huge grand opening on Monday. I'd like to invite you because you've been a big part of this. I'll even let you have any pastry in the case with a coffee. My treat. Please come." She paused, then dropped her voice before whispering, "I miss you."

She hung up the phone. She'd done what she could. Now it was up to him.

CHAPTER TEN

MONDAY MORNING, AND the doors of the new Sweetheart bakery opened to the public. Kelly had stopped at a party-supply store Sunday afternoon and had bought huge bunches of pink and red balloons that she'd grouped and tied around the front room. Megs had been in the kitchen since three that morning baking along with Tom. The display cases overflowed with doughnuts, cookies and coffee cakes. Gina, her cashier, and Kelly bagged and rang up purchases. They also encouraged every customer to enter the drawing for a free month of pastries. Soon the fishbowl was full of entries.

Megs stayed in the kitchen, mixing and baking more recipes, but she could hear the constant beeping of the cash register. A good sign.

She pushed the shortbread dough into the bar pan, then used a fork to poke holes into the smooth surface. The buttery aroma of the dough tickled her nose and she smiled. She was back, better than ever.

Midmorning, Megs took a break from the baking and walked into the front room. Kelly cleaned tables off as Gina rang up another customer. She noted the levels of the baked goods in the display cases. She'd need to bring out more buttermilk doughnuts once Tom finished frying them, and they could use more of the bear claws. "Sounds as though you've been busy out here."

Gina nodded. "Since we opened the doors at seven. Everyone's said how much they've missed us."

"I've had to make about a dozen pots of coffee already." Kelly paused from wiping down the table and put a fist in the small of her back and stretched. "I forgot how much stress this puts on my old body."

"You're barely over thirty." Megs smiled at her sister. "But I appreciate how hard you're working for me."

Kelly grinned and returned to cleaning off the tables. The bell above the front door sounded, and Megs looked up, hoping to see Adam. Instead, Rick Allyn walked in and strode right up to the display case. "Please tell me you have bear claws. I've been craving one for months."

Megs took a piece of tissue and pulled one out of the case for him. She put it in a pastry bag and handed it to him. "No charge, Mr. Mayor. I appreciate everything you did to help all of us."

"Thank you, Megs, but I insist on paying." He pulled out a five-dollar bill and handed it to Gina. "Keep the change." He took the pastry out of the bag and paused. "Don't tell my wife." Then he took a big bite and left the bakery.

Gina rang up the bear-claw purchase and put the remainder of the change into the tip jar next to the register. The jar looked quite full already. "He's probably the fiftieth person to leave a big tip. They've missed us."

Megs nodded and walked to the cash register. She pressed a few buttons, then pulled out money, leaving enough to still make change. She'd get to the bank for their first deposit. She grabbed a pastry box and filled it with doughnuts, as well. "I'll be back in fifteen minutes or so. Anyone need anything while I'm out?"

She took the money in the back, counted it and filled out a deposit slip before putting it in the green bank bag. She put it under her arm and grabbed her coat and purse before walking out the back door. The weather was warming up since the chill of winter, but it was still cold enough to require a coat.

At the bank, she noticed that the parking lot was busy. A good sign for Adam. She parked the car and grabbed the deposit bag and pastry box before walking into the branch. Three people lined up before her at the teller line, so she took her place and waited. When she reached the front, Eva called her over to her window. "More treats?"

"It's our first day open again, so I thought I'd bring some fresh doughnuts over for you." She handed the deposit bag to Eva. "As you can see, it's been a productive morning."

Eva counted the money and nodded. "Everyone's missed you since the bakery's been closed."

"They've missed my pastries, you mean."

Eva paused in her counting and looked up at her. "We can get doughnuts anywhere, including the gas station. People come to the Sweetheart because of you."

"Thank you." She took a deep breath and glanced around. "I left a message for Adam. I'd hoped he'd be able to stop by and see the new and improved bakery, since he fought so hard for it."

Eva pursed her lips and handed her the receipt for the deposit. "He's been on the phone all morning with our district supervisor. Word is he's being promoted and moving to a new location."

Megs turned and glanced at the closed office door. "Adam's leaving?"

"He's been offered the job, but no one knows if he's accepted it yet." Eva sighed. "And I was just getting used to him, too."

"Me, too." Megs thanked Eva again then turned to leave. She kept her eye on the closed office door, but Adam didn't come out as he had before. Didn't wave or smile at her. Instead, the office door remained shut, cutting him off from everyone.

She tried not to take it personally.

ADAM HUNG UP the phone call from Dave and stood. He rubbed away some of the tension that had pooled in his neck. Out his office window, he could see Megan leaving the bank. He should really get over to the Sweetheart, show his support for her business. But he couldn't get motivated to do so.

Dave had pushed hard for him to accept the job offer, but he still had reservations. He'd asked for a few more hours to decide. He needed to be sure that he was not only making the right decision for himself, but for the community, as well.

It would be nice to tell his father to his face about the promotion and ask him who was worthless now. The extra income would also pad his future.

But he didn't want to leave Lake Mildred when he was finally being accepted. He would be leaving it better off than it had been before, but it wasn't enough. The town was on the path to success, but it would be nice to watch the benefits of it. To see the community grow and thrive. To have a hand in harvesting the fruits of his labors these past six months rather than leaving it for a predecessor to step in. He'd also discovered a mentoring relationship with Keegan, giving him a real chance to impact the kid's life for the better. It almost made up for his past.

And then there was Megan. It was time for him to make a decision about her, too.

MEGS RETURNED TO the bakery feeling lower than when she had left. The news of Adam's promotion left an empty spot in her heart that he'd just been starting to fill. She hung up her coat and purse and put on Grammy's favorite pink apron with rainbow-colored butterflies. Maybe if she channeled the spirit of her grandmother, she would know what to do.

She took out the old recipe ledger Grammy had given her weeks before she died. Flipped through pages, looking for something new to try. She paused when she saw Grammy's spidery handwriting next to a recipe. *A cake to start a new relationship.* She read the ingredients and nodded. She had everything she needed.

She gathered the ingredients and sifted the dry ones together. Then she creamed butter, white and brown sugars and eggs together. She let honey drizzle into the mixture and beat the mixture until it was fluffy. Slowly, she added the dry ingredients into the honey-and-sugar mixture, then poured the batter into a small cake pan. She checked the temperature on one of the ovens and slid the pan inside, setting the timer.

As the cake baked, the smell of spices and honey permeated the kitchen. Kelly popped her head inside. "New recipe?"

Megs nodded. "For a special customer."

"Maybe you should have baked two, so we could try it."

"Another time." Megs nodded to the front room. "How are we doing on bread?"

Then it was back to bakery business and not worrying about whether Adam would show or not.

Kelly interrupted her baking and pulled her out into the front room for the arrival of Suzy, followed by Presley, Tori and Shelby. It distracted her momentarily as she came out from the kitchen. "What are you all doing here?"

Presley looked at Suzy, who brought out

a card from behind her back. "We wanted to support you on your big day."

Megs blushed and opened the envelope. The front of the card pictured a train engine winking. Inside, it read, "We knew you could." And it was signed by everyone from the girls' weekend, along with others who hadn't been able to make it.

She held the card to her heart and walked around the counter to give them each a hug in turn. "This means a lot to me."

The door opened, and Page rushed in. "Did you give her the card already? I'm not that late."

Suzy glanced at her watch. "In your world, you're right. You're not." She walked to the display case. "Now, I don't know about anyone else, but I'm in the mood for something sweet." She leaned in to Megs. "Thank you for those cinnamon rolls last week, by the way. I couldn't go another day without my fix."

"Then, you might want to try my babka. It's like a cinnamon roll gave birth to a cake."

Suzy held one finger in the air. "Kelly,

can you wrap one of those up to go? And I'll take a double-chocolate muffin."

The other women oohed and aahed over the items in the display case. Megs turned to Page, who pulled her into a hug. "I may have been late, but I'm no less proud of you. This place looks amazing."

"For a while, I didn't think I'd ever get it back." She looked around, pleased at how her friends filled the space with love and support. She turned back to Page. "I don't know if Kelly told you, but I've been meaning to make an appointment with you. I'm dealing with some things that I can't let go of. And until I do, I feel like I'm stuck."

Page pulled out her cell phone and clicked on the calendar app. "I've got Wednesday afternoons free if the bakery can spare you then."

"Thanks."

"But only if you promise to bring Henry his favorite cheesecake brownies."

"You mean your favorite."

Page shrugged. "Maybe it's both of ours." She clicked some buttons. "I'll see you at four, then. We'll get it all sorted out."

"Thanks."

The two women joined the others as they made their purchases, then took over two tables to eat pastries and drink coffee. They made Megs feel as though it was a party.

And maybe it was.

MEGS FLIPPED THE sign to Closed, but kept her watch on the street outside. Surely he would come even if just to say hi, right? He wouldn't let her first day pass without stopping by. She sighed and turned to find her staff watching her. "Thank you all for your hard work today. Everyone was so happy to see us back in business."

Kelly walked over and handed her the bank bag with the deposit ready for the following morning. "Just needs to be double counted."

"Thanks." Megs looked around the front room. Very few things left to be finished before they could go home. "Why don't you all head home? I can finish up myself."

"I can stay with you. Get us out that much faster," Kelly offered.

Megs waved off her sister's offer. "I need a moment alone before I call it a day."

She wiped down the marble worktable as

her employees gathered their items. Once they left, she locked the back door and turned on the radio to Grammy's favorite country station. She pulled the broom out and swept first the kitchen then the front room as she sang along with the radio. She'd done this job for twelve years, and she still enjoyed it. Still liked ending her day alone with the radio and the broom.

She put the chairs on top of the tables and swept underneath them. Used the broom as a microphone and sang along with the duet asking them to stay the night. Once the sweeping was finished, she brought out the mop and danced across the floor with it. She dipped it then straightened as she heard a knock on the front door. Through the windows, she could see a figure peering inside at her. She shook her head and yelled, "We're closed. We open tomorrow at seven."

"Megan, it's me."

Sure enough, as he backed up, the light from the lamppost outside lit the hard planes of Adam's face. She put the mop in the sudsy bucket and carefully walked over the wet floor to the front door. She unlocked it and opened it an inch. "I'm still closed."

"I know I missed your big day, but I have a good excuse."

Right. The promotion. "Congratulations. Eva told me your good news."

He frowned at her. "The town grapevine is alive and well, I see. But that's not my excuse."

She opened the door wider and ushered him inside. He glanced around the front room and held out his arms. "It came out great. And it smells wonderful."

"It was better earlier." Even though their friendship had been strained since the talent show, she still couldn't believe he hadn't stopped by earlier. He was practically her business partner, yet he hadn't shared in the success of her first day back. She squelched the bitter feelings and held up her hand. "I'll show you around, but be careful. I just mopped in here."

He grinned. "I saw the dance moves."

She rolled her eyes and ushered him behind the display cases that were now empty and ready for the next day's bounty. Walked him to the back and pointed out all the new features, including the gleaming ovens, now cool. "You were able to salvage the marble work island, I see."

"One of the few things I could. My grandparents used it for over fifty years, and I hated the thought that I might lose it. It saved me." She leaned on the counter and looked up at him. "So what's your good excuse?"

"Eva's right about the promotion. It's a huge offer. I'd be managing two branches in the UP."

"That is huge. Like I said, congratulations." She looked back at the cooler where the honey-spice cake waited. "I have something for you. To celebrate."

She went into the cooler and took a deep breath. He was leaving. She'd finally resolved her feelings for him, and he'd be gone. Distance didn't make the heart grow fonder; it made the passion dissipate. She grabbed the cake that she'd drizzled with orange glaze and brought it out with her. She set it in front of him on the marble counter. "It's one of my grandmother's recipes."

She pulled drawers until she found the

silverware and took out a fork and handed it to Adam. "Unless you'd rather take it home."

"You made this for me?" He took the fork and plunged it through one side, pulling out a sizable piece. He brought it up to his face and first smelled it, then put it in his mouth. Megs watched him as he chewed slowly, then closing his eyes.

"Is it good?"

"It tastes like how I imagine my future. One with you in it." He opened his eyes and took another forkful of the cake. He fed the bite to her, then put the fork on the counter and pulled her into a kiss. He tasted like the cake, spicy and sweet. He framed her face with his hands as he kissed her, pulling her into a swirl of emotions. This was right. This was wrong. This was good.

She pushed against his chest. "Wait." She tried to catch her breath. "What about your promotion?"

"My work here isn't finished."

The thought of him staying made her smile, but then it faded. "I don't know about this."

"You still don't know what you want?"

Adam took a step back. "Let me tell you what I want. I want to stop thinking about you every day and dreaming about you every night. Because living in this town and not being with you is driving me crazy. I can't keep doing it." He gestured at her than at himself. "You and I make a good team. Together, we held a successful fund-raiser that made thousands of dollars for the town. We brought back the Sweetheart. And we could make an amazing partnership as a couple. There'd be no stopping us."

Megs's head swam not only with the kiss but his declaration. He loved her. He may not have said it in so many words, but he loved and wanted her. She who couldn't be loved. Who everyone left. He'd offered her everything she wanted. All she had to do was agree. To hold out her hand and accept him as he was now, letting go of the boy he'd been. Just as he took her now, releasing the girl who had failed.

He put his hands on her shoulders. "Just let go, Megs. I won't let you fall."

"Yes." The word came out soft as a whisper. She nodded and said it louder. "Yes."

Adam looked into her eyes. "You're sure?"

Then again, even louder. "Yes. A thousand times, yes." She fell into his arms, and he caught her and held her there.

ADAM DROVE THEM to the cemetery a few weeks later on a sunny Saturday that held the hint of spring. He parked alongside the curb, then hurried to the other side to help Megs down from the truck. She clasped the bouquet of brightly colored helium balloons tightly in her fist. He reached out and pushed a golden strand of hair from her eyes. "You're sure you want to do this?"

"It was Page's idea, and she's usually right." She handed him two of the balloons and started walking across the hill to Kenny's grave site. She knelt in the grass and plucked at the few dead weeds that obscured the stone with his name. "Hey, Kenny. We're here, even though I know it's months before the anniversary. I hope you're resting in peace now. I'm sorry I haven't come sooner."

Adam knelt next to her and took her free hand in his.

"I couldn't save you. I realize that now.

I miss you every day. But something good, something really good has happened." She squeezed Adam's hand. "He's back and he's a good man. Still, I can't give him my heart until I tell you..." Several minutes passed before she could say the words. "Goodbye, Kenny."

She and Adam stood, hands still joined, and set free the balloons. They watched them float away slowly, bobbing as the wind blew them over the trees and became dots in the distance as they rose higher in the sky.

Adam put his arm around Megs's shoulder. "Have I told you today how much I love you?"

She put her arm around his waist. "Not yet. But I expect you to make it up to me."

Together, they walked to the truck. Because together, they could do anything. Even let go of the past and create a future.

* * * * *